Through the Shadows

a paranormal romance

Gloria Teague

DIVA

Denton, Texas

This is a work of fiction. Names, characters, places, and incidents are products of the author's imagination or are used fictitiously and are not to be construed as real. Any resemblance to actual events, locales, organizations, or persons, living or dead, is entirely coincidental.

DIVA
An imprint of AWOC.COM Publishing
P.O. Box 2819
Denton, TX 76202

Manufactured in the United States of America

ISBN: 978-1-62016-004-6

Visit the author's website: http://www.gloriateague.com

Chapter One

"It'd be easier to make money as a stripper in a smoke-filled, bug infested bar. Too bad I threw out all my fishnet hose. Too bad I don't have the body for it. Too bad I can't dance." Tori sighed, glanced over the last sentence written, and let her fingers fly across the keyboard.

He pulled Helene close, then closer still. Burying his nose in the luxuriant, flaxen curls clinging damply to her neck, Avery gently nibbled his way to the hollow of her throat and felt his lover's pulse quicken against his lips.

Helene's breathing grew rapid and shallow, her chest rose more with each breath as her passion grew. Her slender fingers drew his head closer to her. As he began to slowly, so slowly, kiss the hollow at her throat, she stroked the coarse, thick mat on his chest.

Helene enjoyed the way the moonlight had cast glints of silver within his jet black hair and ran her fingers through the soft tresses. She moved her hands across his back; the fingernails pressed just hard enough to leave a trail of tingles down his spine.

Avery pulled her to him, crushing her breasts against his hard chest, eliciting a moan through her parted lips. Her head fell back and her eyes were glazed in wanton desire.

Avery's own passion grew stronger by the second as he pulled the plunging neckline of her dress to her waist. Avery's breath caught at her perfection and leaned down to...

"No, no, no! What's wrong with you, you idiot? When did you start writing *bodice rippers*?" Talking to herself sometimes helped pull her thoughts into focus. "That's too forceful for Avery! He would never rip a lady's gown, even if she invited him to. C'mon Tori, you can write better than this crap!"

She shook her head at the character's lack of finesse, and then realized it was her own lack of style. Tori was disappointed in herself for writing such a thing.

The corners of her lips were turned down in concentration, trying to correct this terrible wrong she had done her protagonist. She hated to go back and rewrite the whole chapter but she saw no way around it. She pulled her bottom lip between her teeth to chew on it thoughtfully. What to do, what to do?

She felt a soft kiss of frosty air drift across the back of her neck with a feather-like touch and a chill skittered down her spine. Nerve-endings were screaming a warning to the brain and her throat became arid. Tori stared at the computer screen, straining her peripheral vision to see who stood behind her. Whoever it was stood close enough that she could feel the heaviness of the air being occupied by his mass.

Did I leave the door open? Oh man, I didn't bother to set the alarm. Glancing over the surface of her deck, Tori saw she had nothing to use as a weapon. Quickly, she envisioned the layout of the room, the house, trying to quell her pounding heart enough to plan a route of escape.

I can plant my feet on the floor and forcefully shove my chair straight back, right into whoever it is. The weight of my body should be enough to at least knock him down. Him. Why am I thinking it's a HIM? Because, O God, a murderer would be a big strong man! But, maybe, with the element of surprise... O God, O God, O God! Okay, now just stop it! Just take a deep breath and do it before it's too late. DO IT NOW!

Feet firmly planted, Tori leaned forward in her chair, then slammed her body against the back of the chair while shoving off with her feet. She held her breath, waiting for the collision and the terror of what would happen next.

Her chair tipped over, her legs flung outward like a wishbone, her hands scrabbled at empty air, trying to find purchase, and she cracked her head on the doorknob of the closet where she kept her writing supplies. Even through the swirling, bright stars dancing in front of her eyes, she could see there was no one there.

Well Tori, you've finally lost it! Mom always said if you keep writing "this stuff" you'll lose your mind. Mom's gonna be so happy that she was right.

She pulled herself off the floor, righted her chair, and rubbed the back of her head to feel the small knot already forming. She sat down straighter in her chair, turning her head to work the kinks from her neck and shoulders. The joints creaked and groaned like protesting hinges of a long-locked door being opened. Getting lost in your writing was a sure bet for muscle soreness. *And throwing yourself against a wooden door was another. Perhaps a healthy imagination isn't so healthy, after all.*

Get away from the computer, at least for a few minutes. Stretch out, get a cup of coffee, think about something other than this damned book for a few minutes. It's no wonder Jim left! How could he cope with an absentee wife living in Fantasy Land? I seem to forget there is another world, the real world, out there. It's just so much easier to be in the company of people that I have created. I know what they're thinking, and how they're feeling, every minute. I determine what my characters do for a living, who they marry, and how many children they have. I even make the decision if they live or die. It's a tough act for real people to follow. Even close friends pale by comparison to fictional characters, and it doesn't take them too long to figure that out.

Tori Stanfield—Writer Extraordinaire! No husband, no children, no friends, only a mother and an agent who refuse to give up on me. Thank God for families!

Tori decided against putting on the kettle she used for making decaffeinated coffee. This was going to be a long and hopefully productive night; she needed all the caffeine she could get. She heard a low, grumbling sound as she measured the coffee. She grinned when she realized it was her stomach, complaining because she had forgotten to eat-again.

It never ceases to amaze me how I can forget the most mundane but important things, like eating. I know that's bad, but it does keep me in a size three! But a size three is kinda skinny stretched out on a five-five frame, I suppose. I guess I better grab a sandwich before my gut starts talking to me.

The emptiness of the house suddenly seemed oppressive. As she stood in the kitchen trying to convince herself to eat, Tori felt the silence weighing down upon her. Slapping together ham-and-cheese on rye and calling it good, she walked over to turn on the CD player.

The sounds of Motown were instantly soothing as she cranked up the volume. The sixties music comforted her like an old friend. Even if she *did* have friends, they'd make fun of her for liking music that was older than she was. She danced around the floor, dropping breadcrumbs and singing in an enthusiastic, even if off-key, voice. The next CD of various artists was mellow and made her smile between bites.

She stopped in mid-step and mid-note as the music died. There had been a noise like a hammer-blow and the CD stopped spinning. The lights of the equalizer no longer flickered in rhythm and the power switch light was off. Vertical lines knitted themselves between her perfectly plucked eyebrows.

Tori stomped across the floor, flipped her long red hair over her shoulder and glared at the stereo with green eyes squinted. She repeatedly punched the power button and when she received no positive reaction to her technological probing, she gave the wooden case a swift kick.

"Well, isn't that just great? Isn't it absolutely wonderful? Stupid, stupid stereo! I can't afford to have it fixed. Not now. But someday... Someday I'm gonna be rich and famous, and I'll just throw away anything that doesn't work. Right! I won't even bother to have it repaired. Yeah, sure! And when I'm rich and famous I can also afford therapy for talking to myself!"

Shrugging, Tori took her coffee and half-eaten sandwich back to work with her. Some people would have called this room an office, or a study, but she called it simply "the room of dreams."

Tori loved her old house that had been built in the early fifties. With over two thousand square feet it was much too big for her, but she didn't mind. When she and Jim had bought the house, it had been with the idea of having children to fill the rooms. The house sat in the middle of a huge parcel of farmland, complete with wooden fences. There were even a few water troughs left from the previous owner.

There were several rooms that she never used. The house had two living areas, four bedrooms, and two baths. She used one bedroom, leaving two spare rooms in case she ever had any company. The smallest one she had converted into a writing room. It held her computer, a large desk, and several bookcases filled with research books.

It had been fun finding information about the different eras of history and she had managed to assemble quite an assortment of reference books. In the early years, she had found that most people scoffed at the idea of romantic fantasy. At that time, not only did these people not believe in any such thing, they refused to buy books about it, either, which was too bad for her because that was what her novels were all about. True, they were all fiction, but she thought they were good, solid pieces of work. Now that the historical romance genre was taking off, Tori was selling more books, just not enough to repair an out-dated stereo. One day she'd hit it big, she just knew it. Until that day she would keep plodding along, selling as many copies as die-hard romantics would buy.

Tori was rational enough to realize she lived her romantic fantasies through her writing. Her lonely life was made more bearable by creating her dream man, her one true love. He was the leading character in the series of books she had written.

His name was Avery Norcross and he was everything Tori dreamed of in a man. She knew that no mere mortal could possibly live up to the high standards she had created for him.

As she stared into her fantasy world that Avery inhabited, she could see his heart-stopping visage in her mind's eye: His long, thick mane of jet-black hair blowing in the wind, tugging to be free of the leather strip that held it. He was stopped at the top of a grassy knoll, astride the sweating, massive body of his chestnut mount, Mankala. The steed was prancing from one hoof to another, snorting in annoyance at being held at bay.

Avery's strong chin was lifted; his eyes, an icy aquamarine of the open sea, scanning the countryside for anyone foolish enough to trespass the grounds of the Norcross land. The moonlight cascaded over his strong, broad shoulders and flat belly. Tori imagined the muscles of Avery's thighs tensing against the movement of the horse. She held her breath, almost as if in anticipation of a loving caress from this beautiful, *fictional*, man.

As she sat with her chin in her hand, the computer screen-saver kicked in and moved across her face in kaleidoscopic colors. Gazing into the face of a man that she longed for with every part of her being, she jumped from her chair as The Temptations' "Just My Imagination" rocked back into existence.

Oh, very appropriate!

The usually smooth, laid-back sounds that reminisced the days of flower power and free love crashed over her in a cacophony of blistering noise. Tori slapped her hands over her ears as she ran to the stereo to turn down the ear-splitting volume. Just as her fingers touched the control, the whole system shut itself down again.

"You lousy piece of junk! Scare me half to death! I could've had a heart attack, you crummy, no-good..."

Muttering to herself, Tori reached for the electrical cord. She viciously jerked on the cord, pulling the entire outlet from the wall.

"There! That'll do it! *Now* let's see if you can blast my blood pressure into stroke range again."

Tori walked back to the computer, dusting her hands off as she settled back into her chair and stared into space. After a few minutes, she decided the caffeine wasn't working and neither was her brain, so she might as well go to bed.

She was mourning the loss of the stereo as she brushed her teeth. For years she had left it on at night, the soft music playing background noise so she wouldn't notice the silence. Even now, she laughed at the irony that she claimed to fear nothing—but needed a radio to chase the boogeyman away while she slept. She had tried leaving the television on at night, but the constant change in volume from program to commercials kept her awake.

Oh well, Tori, I guess you'll go cold turkey tonight. No smooth sounds from Al Green or soulful tunes from Smokey Robinson to keep you company.

She turned down the duvet on her double bed that tonight seemed mammoth and slid between the cool, crisp sheets. Staring into the imageless void, Tori realized this was the first time she had noticed how truly dark it was in her room. Disgusted, she got out of bed to turn on the bathroom light but forced herself to show some maturity and close the door partway.

I may need to get up to go to the bathroom in the middle of the night. I don't want to bump into anything in the dark.

The bed wasn't as comforting as it had been a few minutes before. The pillow now had canyon-sized craters, no matter how much she tried to fluff it out. The mattress developed boulder-sized lumps and the sheets were trying to grasp her legs in a stranglehold.

The house picked this time to act up, too. Every wooden beam began to creak like an old-man's joints. The windowpanes rattled like dry bones in their frames. From the bathroom there was the roaring, monotonous drip of a water faucet.

Gawd! This is ridiculous! I may as well admit defeat and turn on the television. I'm not going to be able to go to sleep in all this noisy silence!

Sneering at her own cowardice, Tori stalked into the living room to turn on the television. She thought the best choice would be a music channel but all the local cable company offered was a country music station.

"Oh well, it's better than nothing. Yee haw! Ride 'em cowboy!"

As she was leaving the room, she stopped just long enough to switch on one of the lamps beside the couch.

Chicken!

Tori walked into the kitchen to make a cup of coffee and saw the indicator light was bright on the coffee maker, telling her she had forgotten to turn it off. She poured herself a cup and decided it wasn't too strong, even after sitting there for two hours.

Only two hours? Strange, it seems much longer than that. I guess it's a good a thing ironing clothes is against my religion. I'd probably leave the iron on, too, and burn the house down around my head!

She carried her cup into the living room, debating if she wanted to force herself to work on her book or lose herself in some meaningless, late-night television program. She knew that she didn't do her best writing if she wasn't in the mood, so she opted for the TV.

While channel surfing, she found one her favorite movies was on. She leaned back in her recliner, sipped her coffee, and became enmeshed in the story. She had always enjoyed the movie, not only for its knighted men, but also for their undying love for their ladies. Tori had often wished she had a man to love her like that. He would battle for her, give his life for her, but not before he loved her completely and thoroughly. But Tori knew that even if she were ready for love again, her own imaginative mind would keep most men far away. She had her own painful past to draw from to reach that conclusion.

* * *

Tori had wanted to be a writer since she was twelve years old. She began writing short stories about anything and everything. She could hear a song title or a particularly picturesque phrase, and just sit still, allowing her imagination free reign. She could travel the span of this world and imagined others in her mind. Different scenarios would jockey and shift into position, only to be replaced by a bigger, better idea. Within minutes, a full-fledged story took up residence and she would begin frantically writing before she lost the idea.

Words had always been her best friends, her own creativity drawing her into its lonely, alluring grip. When her mind was filled with words begging to be written, there weren't enough hours in the day to keep up, and friends fell by the wayside.

One of the few exceptions to this rule was Jim Stanfield, a young man she met at a coffee shop. He had seen something special deep inside the shy girl, her loving heart beneath the seemingly aloof exterior. Others had thought her standoffish, but Jim had seen the truth.

The marriage had been serene, comforting, and Tori's love for writing took a backseat to the love for her husband. The fact that she was not writing wasn't a hardship; she knew that she could return to it any time she wished. She just felt it best to give herself completely to Jim, at least for a few years.

They had bought this house, decorating it with playful enthusiasm. Just picking out the wallpaper had been an adventure for the two lovebirds. They took their time remodeling, even decorating a room for the nursery with confidant love.

Tori had never used birth control; she and Jim both wanted a baby as soon as possible. Each month was a disappointment that was tempered with hope that the next month would be a joyful victory. In the beginning, they explained it away by saying they were trying too hard, she hadn't been ovulating at the right time, or they were too tensed-up about the situation.

As the months turned into years, the disappointment turned to anger and they both became bitter. They began quarreling about unimportant things, like what to have for dinner. Soon the arguments turned ugly. Jim blamed her for not becoming pregnant and Tori blamed him for not being fertile enough to *get* her pregnant.

It all ended just before Christmas, five years before. The fight started over what kind of tree they would buy to decorate. It escalated into a screaming, cursing battle they would both remember for the rest of their lives. When Jim walked out she spent that Christmas, and every one after that, without him.

It took Tori several months to realize Jim was never coming home. She now accepted it, but she had never quit hurting. She also accepted the fact that the kind of love she wanted, needed, would never be hers.

Loneliness had enveloped her soul like a shroud. To accelerate the healing process, Tori had gone back to her one constant, true friend—writing. She thought if she lost herself in words that she wouldn't miss Jim so much. All she had accomplished was making a little money so she could survive. She took it one day at a time, praying her heart would mend.

Sharon, her mother, had been a blessing. If not for her, Tori felt she wouldn't have made it. She had moved in with her daughter until the worst of the storm had passed and only a quiet light mist remained. Sharon had then gone back home but stayed in frequent contact with her only child. Tori knew that her mother prayed every day for her to find a cure for her bruised heart.

The answer to Sharon's prayers for her daughter came in the form of a literary agent. Lydia Palmer was a strong force to be reckoned with but she had a soft spot for new, promising writers. The intimidating Brit became Tori's agent, critic, and friend. Lydia had taken Tori's raw talent and helped polish it to a dazzling diamond just waiting to be discovered.

It was Lydia who encouraged Tori when the rejections poured in. It was Lydia who helped construct a foundation to boost Tori's meager sense of self-worth. It was Lydia who encouraged the young writer to never give up, to keep fighting. For these priceless gifts, Tori would always love and respect her agent.

Over the years, Lydia had become like family to Tori and Sharon. The older women seem to have a special connection and their friendship grew into a sisterhood.

As she stared without interest at the television, Tori smiled when she thought about Lydia joining her for lunch in just a few hours. She knew she would look bedraggled from lack of sleep and grinned when she imagined how Lydia would be concerned, but understanding. Lydia, too, had been left by a husband and had floundered alone in a tidal wave of loneliness. Perhaps that's the reason her career had taken on such a frantic edge.

So intent on her thoughts, Tori didn't hear the muffled step in the adjoining room. A soft, seductive voice spoke her name. It asked her when she was coming to bed. The voice, tone, and timber were so real, so *intimate*, she momentarily forgot Jim wasn't there anymore. A familiar feeling of loving amusement that he had felt for her side of the bed, found it empty and wanted her to come to bed, made her grin. And, just as always, she answered him.

"Just a minute, honey."

In the space of a heartbeat she remembered, and was terrified.

Her breath caught in her chest, her ears strained for any and every sound. Her eyes were round and large as she stared straight ahead, afraid to turn her head in the direction of the voice. Terror drummed through her veins and she felt the accompanying pulse at her temple.

Trembling, her head rotated on its axis and Tori could hear every vertebrae grind in the terminally slow movement. The elasticity of her skin seemed to have shrunken into a sweat-drenched mask, too tight to allow an expression.

Tori didn't want to (*had to, had to*) look into the dark (*O God, it's so dark in there!*) hallway. Every fiber of her numb brain implored her to just get the hell out of there. But where could she go, at 3 A.M., in pajamas, and with her keys in her purse, *in the other room?*

Oh, this is ridiculous! I'm thirty years old and I'm afraid of some little sound in my own home? Okay, okay, it's more than just a sound and if I'm honest with myself, I'll admit I'm scared to pieces. O God, what a horrible, grotesque expression. I don't think I'll use that particular phrase ever again. All right, stop it, Tori. Right now. Get up off your duff and see where that noise came from.

Not any braver for her own pep talk, Tori forced herself to stand up. Taking as deep a breath as frozen lungs would allow, she whirled on her heel, ready to run if necessary.

There was no one there. It was just as earlier that evening, in the computer room, when she thought she had felt a presence behind her. Was she losing her ever-loving mind? Was it really time for an extended vacation in a Rubber Ramada where all the mattresses were nailed to the wall?

Tori's explosive release of breath came from the pit of her stomach. Mentally shaking her head, she gave into the shiver that jittered between her shoulders.

Tori heated her cold coffee in the microwave then went back to her old comfortable chair. She steadily increased the volume of the television, covering up the silence. She didn't have to worry about disturbing the neighbors—she didn't have any. The only protesters would be the small animals playing tag in the dirt and gravel driveway.

Artificial, canned laughter filled the rooms of the too-large house, sweeping cobwebs from the dusty corners. Tori leaned back in the recliner, coaxing the footrest to come out of hiding. Each passing, uneventful minute brought a decrease in her heart rate. She started to question her own hearing, her own logic, at last convincing herself either she hadn't heard what she thought she had, or it was on the television.

She spotted a bottle on the table next to her chair. *Maybe I'll just pop a Benadryl, get a little drowsy and then go to bed.*

Television infomercials took up the next forty-five minutes. She shifted into neutral and the spinning wheels of her brain slowed to an idling phase. Her purple-shadowed eyelids grew leaden. Less than an hour after her gut-wrenching terror, Tori was snoring softly. She never heard the mournful sigh echo throughout the house.

Chapter Two

A persistent, annoying pounding crashed through the delightful dream Tori was smiling through. Groggily, she opened her eyes, only to be momentarily blinded by fierce, radiant beams of sunlight falling through the window. She rubbed her eyes like a small child, still wearing a grin which dissolved with the next series of hammer-blows on the front door.

Tori glanced at the clock next to the TV as she climbed out of the chair.

Wow, I can't believe I slept that long.

Without looking to see who the impolite, irritating person was on the other side, she pulled the door open.

Her hair was a wind-tossed bird's nest and she was shifting papers to keep her claim on them, Lydia glared at Tori.

"Oh. My. God! It's eleven o'clock and you're still asleep! Great. I went to all the trouble of making lunch reservations and now we won't get there on time. Wonderful, Tori, just bloody wonderful!"

Tori threw her arms around her disgruntled friend and pulled her into the room. She lightly kissed Lydia's cheek as she closed the door.

"Good morning, dear, sweet, *understanding*, Lydia. I'm so happy to see your bright, cheerful face."

Lydia Palmer struggled to maintain the look of stern disapproval for her young client's behavior.

"Don't start with me, Victoria Lynn Stanfield! Good thing I told you I'd pick you up for lunch or you would've stood me up—again. I know it's tough being a writer but you absolutely have to get your priorities straight. Stop that insane grinning,

will you? *Mon Dios*, you're driving me to drink! Speaking of which, be a dear and fix me a screwdriver, okay, love?"
Tori laughed merrily. She leaned over to pinch the agent's cheek and Lydia tried, in vain, to slap the hand away.
"Now, now, Lydia! Play nice. A screwdriver? At eleven o'clock in the morning? Kinda early, isn't it?"
Lydia expelled air through her surgically perfect nose.
"Some of us do not sleep away an entire day, Tori. Some of us get up very early and have accomplished many important things by eleven o'clock in the morning. Besides, a screwdriver has orange juice, a regular breakfast beverage. Okay? Now stop acting like my mother and fix your agent a nice drink."
Tori spun on her heel and headed for the kitchen to start a pot of coffee. Lydia wouldn't be too happy about it but that was just too bad. Tori knew her friend disliked American coffee and only drank tea, when she could be persuaded to drink anything non-alcoholic. This morning, though, Miss Snooty wasn't going to get her way. It was going to be coffee or nothing.
Lydia kept up a steady stream of conversation as Tori measured coffee grounds in the filter. She could imagine her friend's words, had she been in the room with her.
Really, Victoria! Perked coffee? For God's sake, don't you at least have an espresso machine?
Tori carried the coffee into the living room and Lydia frowned when she saw the aromatic steam rising from the cup. Tori grinned and Lydia's lips puckered in a pout.
"Tori, love, you know I hate coffee."
"Yes, my dear Lydia, but that's all that's available in this house. Now, be a good girl and drink up while I take a quick shower. I'll be ready in 20 minutes."
Lydia took the proffered cup, refusing to meet Tori's eyes.
"You know, Tori, you're not my mother. And you really should forget this notion you have that I drink too much."
Tori smirked, then shuffled toward the bathroom.
In the living room, Lydia opened her Louis Vuitton bag. While watching the hallway for signs of Tori, she surreptitiously pulled a silver flask from her purse. The lid rattled against the glass and she quickly removed it. She may

hate American coffee but never let it be said she hated Irish coffee.

The women continued their conversation across the hallway. Tori was pulling on her sweater and jeans as Lydia sipped her now-acceptable coffee.

"So, Lydia, where are we having lunch?"

Lydia gulped the swallow she held in her mouth so she could answer and swore as the hot coffee scalded her throat.

"Bloody hell!"

"What? I didn't hear you. Where did you say?"

Lydia dabbed at her smeared lipstick and again reached for the bottle.

"We're eating at The Fountain."

Tori sighed then pulled her sweater over her head and jerked down the zipper of her jeans. She duck-walked to the closet; the jeans still wrapped around her ankles. She lifted one leg free and sailed the pants across the room with her other foot. She scraped hangers across the metal rod in her closet, trying to find a dress suitable for the restaurant Lydia had chosen for lunch. Tori would've been happier with fast food but Lydia would have been horrified at such a thought.

She rummaged through the dresser drawers, looking for a pair of stockings with the least runs, muttering to herself. The best pair she found had no runs but there was a rip in the crotch.

Well, it's the best I can do. With any luck, they won't rip any more. Where'd I put my clear fingernail polish?

Tori covered the entire ripped seam with the acrylic polish then blew on them to speed the drying process.

"Why The Fountain, Lydia? Couldn't you have chosen something a little less elegant? Good grief! It's only lunch!"

Tori could just imagine Lydia rolling her eyes toward the ceiling as if imploring someone to give her strength to not yell at her young, unsophisticated writer.

"Well, love, we're having a guest for lunch. An important guest, and I thought it terribly inappropriate to ask him to eat a kiddy's meal!"

Tori walked into the living room and lifted her eyebrows at the flask sitting on the end table next to her agent.

"If I'm forced to drink this swill I have to make it more civilized. Coffee, indeed!"

Lydia dropped the alcohol back into her purse, not bothering to make any further excuses for herself.

"A guest? Who is it, Lydia?"

Lydia grinned and Tori recognized the look. It was the expression Lydia wore when she had successfully pulled off a great coup.

"It's your next publisher, Tori. His name is Ted Woodward and he's the acquisition editor for one of the biggest houses in New York! Isn't this exciting?"

Tori was always amazed at Lydia's confidence. She didn't doubt for one moment that this publisher would be interested in Tori's work.

"Lydia! You just automatically assume this man will want to publish my book?"

The agent stood in front of Tori and smiled as she smoothed the young woman's stray wisps of hair.

"No, love, I don't doubt it. You are very talented, Tori, and this man will see that. Not only will he publish this next book but he will be begging to publish each one of your books after that."

Tori quickly hugged her agent and tears shimmered in her eyes.

"I wish I had as much faith in me as you do, Lydia."

"One day you will, sweet Tori. Now, hurry it up! We're going to dazzle this man, but it may be more difficult if we show up an hour late!"

She swatted Tori with her purse as she rushed her to the front door.

* * *

Lunch with Lydia was always a learning experience for Tori. She watched the beautiful agent work her magic on the editor. She charmed and wooed the distinguished looking man, winning him over completely. She had brought along the partial for Tori's next book. At first, Ted Woodward seemed eager to read it but he only gave it a cursory glance before he told them he would look forward to reading the completed manuscript.

As they were parting at the entrance to the restaurant, he shook Tori's clammy hand and kissed Lydia's cheek.

"Tori, it was a pleasure to meet you. After all of Lydia's glowing praise, I wondered if your work could live up to it. Lydia, are we still on for dinner this evening? Ladies, it has been a delight!"

Tori was wondering just how much her written words had swayed this man's opinion and how much it had been Lydia's voluptuous figure. Either way, she had a tentative publishing contract with one of the largest houses in the business!

On the highway leading back to her house, Tori turned to the agent with a mischievous smile playing around the corners of her lips.

"Lydia! You sneaky little devil, you! How long has this been going on?"

Lydia glanced over with rounded eyes, an expression of assumed innocence at the implied charge of consorting with the enemy.

"Why, Victoria! Whatever do you mean? There's nothing 'going on,' as you so rudely put it! Ted Woodward and I have only known each other for a few days. I contacted him by phone to discuss your book. In the course of the conversation, he just happened to say he thought I had a sexy voice and that he just simply loves the English accent. So I casually mentioned that, perhaps, we should meet in person to discuss my young lady's work. We've had dinner a couple of times, during which I persuaded him to meet with you."

"Lydia, you are one, sly fox!"

Tori's loving smirk did not escape Lydia's notice.

"Now you just mind your manners, Missy! What do you say to going by to see your mother? It's been a few days since we've talked and I miss her. Besides, we simply must tell her the news in person!"

Without waiting for a reply from Tori, Lydia pressed the accelerator a bit harder, seeming to be in a hurry to reach Sharon's house. But then, Lydia was always in a hurry.

Tori smiled, thinking how truly lucky she was. Not only did she get a top-notch agent who had become a loyal friend, but her mother gained a soul mate. The friendship between her mother and her agent always made Tori feel warm inside. It was nice to know that her two staunchest defenders were the best of friends.

In fact, Sharon Canon saw more of her agent than Tori did. They had dinner together and went on long, exhausting shopping excursions for hours on end. The two women often stopped by Tori's after a day spent together, just to show her things they had purchased on their recent mall safari. They would joke and giggle like schoolgirls when they were together. They would unabashedly discuss the men they dated, causing Tori to blush furiously and beg them to stop. Sharon and Lydia would both laugh and only make her blush more.

Lydia pulled the car to the curb and Sharon was standing on the front steps to welcome them before they even got out of the car. She kissed her daughter's cheek and hugged her best friend before escorting them into the house. Immediately, the two older women began their companionable chattering, being so in synch with one another that they would often finish the other's sentence.

"Well, Lydia, what have you and my baby..."

"...been up to? Oh, nothing important. Only meeting with the acquisition editor of a well-known, verrrry prestigious, publishing house. His name's Ted Woodward and he's..."

"...from New York! What did he say? Is he interested in Tori's next book? Oh, how silly! Of course..."

"...he's interested! He's read the synopsis and the first three chapters. He told us he wants to see the rest of the manuscript, right away! Isn't that..."

"...wonderful! Oh baby, I'm so proud of you! Not surprised, though! We know you're a good writer and we were just waiting for someone else to know it, too. Right, Lydia?"

"Absolutely! Let's have a drink to celebrate!"

As Sharon fixed them a martini, she turned to her friend with a sly smile.

"Okay, Lydia, confess! Just what did you do, or promise to do, to get Mr. Big Shot Editor to come here?"

The pretended look of innocence was less convincing than before.

"What is it with you people? Tori asked me the same bloody question!"

Sharon chuckled, then draped an arm around Lydia's shoulders.

"Could it be, just maybe, that Tori and I know you pretty well?"

Adopting a fairly good Southern drawl, Lydia shook her head at them.

"Y'all thank yor sa smart, don't cha?"

Tori laughed so hard she had to hold her stomach. Sharon grinned as she shook her head at Lydia.

The rest of the afternoon was spent discussing the editor, the next book, men in general, and sex in particular. When Tori's face felt it had reached a broiling temperature, she held up her hands in defeat.

"Okay, okay, okay. You guys win. I can't keep up my end of the conversation so I might as well go home."

Lydia, by now feeling the effects of an afternoon of gin, slipped into the cockney accent she had paid to lose.

"Naw, love, you can't. Litl' gulls like you shouldn't even try."

"Well, *ladies*, it could be because I haven't been around as many blocks as you."

Mother and agent both laughed uproariously. One of the things Tori thought was so special about these two women was their sense of humor.

"Lydia, don't even try to say you're taking me home. I'll call a cab. I don't want you behind the wheel of a car. Stay here with Mom and drink about three gallons of coffee before you leave."

"Coffee? Oh my gawd! I can't stand that garbage and you know it!"

Tori giggled. She gave the cab company the address and went to sit with the two most important people in her life until the taxi arrived.

* * *

Sharon and Lydia were still laughing and joking when the cab driver tapped the car horn. Tori kissed both of them but she wasn't sure if they even noticed she was leaving. When she left her mother's house she wore a cloak of familial love that kept her warm.

The taxi driver was in a talkative mood. The only thing required to keep up her end of the conversation was an occasional murmur from Tori. The closer they got to her house, the less she answered, until the driver was answering his own witty questions. When they arrived, Tori paid the driver then stood on the sidewalk that led up to the house that waited for her. For a few seconds Tori felt that her home looked sinister and foreboding.

That's just silly, Tori. This is home, your sanctuary, your soft place to fall and hide from the world. I just wish... oh, I don't know what I wish anymore.

Mentally berating herself didn't alter her mood.

She stared into the empty windows, a deep longing washing over her. She seldom left the house and this desperate loneliness at her return was probably the reason. No matter how much she might dream, or write those dreams on paper, she still had to face facts.

This is reality, Tori. At least, it's your reality. There's never going to be a husband throwing open the door to say, "Hi, honey, I'm home!" There's never going to be the sound of little feet running to greet Daddy.

Tori stared at the sidewalk as she shuffled to the door. Patchwork leaves rattled crisply under her slow step. She stared at the key in her hand for several seconds before sliding it into the lock. The door creaked inward.

She stood on the weathered boards of the porch and stared into the empty void of her life. She stepped into the entryway, closing the door softly behind her.

In an effort to lighten her own heavy heart, Tori shouted into the silence of her home.

"Okay, stop me now if you've heard this one. Did you hear the one about two jumper cables walking into a bar and the bartender said, "Don't you two start anything in here. Get it? Jumper cables? Start something..."

Not even an echo.

"Gee, tough crowd tonight!"

Tori dropped her jacket on the back of the couch. She walked into the dining room and put both hands on the back of a chair, leaning heavily into the wood. Her head hung low, one crystal tear slipped down her ivory cheek.

In the dark recesses of the corner there stood a witness to this display. Without form or texture, the being struggled to be heard. In a voice that could not be detected by the human ear, the entity spoke.

Welcome home, Victoria.

Chapter Three

Tori made a sandwich for herself and another of the endless pots of coffee she drank while writing. Last night had proved to be a dismal failure, so she *had* to make up for it tonight. She'd always heard that to be an accomplished writer, you should write at least one page a day. Normally, she had no trouble whatsoever doing just that. Most days saw the completion of ten pages or more. Yesterday had been a bust and she hadn't written one single word she could keep. She vowed to herself that tonight would be different.

Tori wasn't easily distracted, so she was angry with herself that she imagined all sorts of things that go bump in the night. She now believed it only an excuse to get out of writing and justify it to herself, which was pretty lame, since she answered to no one else when it came to the business of writing.

Tori assembled all her normal equipment following her usual writing protocol. Many writers went through their own type of a superstitious ritual before they began to work and Tori was no different. She had her coffee mug to the right of the keyboard. Her dictionary and thesaurus were to the left (none of this website research for her!) and an orange Tennessee Vols baseball cap on her head honoring her favorite college team. Go Big Orange!

"Alrighty, I'm ready. O great and powerful Oz! Come! Fill me with my own brand of bologna so I can put it on paper."

Staring at the wall above the video monitor, Tori jutted her chin forward in anticipation. She threw her hands up in the air and shrugged her shoulders.

"I'm waiting!"

She held her hands curled over the keyboard, ready to begin typing. An idea flashed through her mind and just as quickly skated away.

"Oh man! I lost it! And I bet it would've been a great idea, too."

Elbow on her desk, Tori leaned her face against her hand, then leaned forward and lightly bounced her head on the computer monitor.

She sat up straight and held her arms out in surrender.

"O Great Gods of Words, don't fail me now! Send a writing spirit to help me. Yeah, a ghostwriter! Wow! That would be cool!"

But no one answered her cry for help even though Tori stared at the video screen for almost two hours. During those long hours her mind wandered in and out of reality. This is how she got her ideas, her inspiration. But the grassy fields she walked through in her mind yielded no brilliant story lines tonight.

Tori was so intent upon her daydreaming that she didn't notice the approaching darkness. When she pulled herself from her imaginary trip, the room was deep in darkness. Quickly, before she had time to think about being afraid, she turned on her desk lamp. She looked through the open doorway behind her and the quiet darkness seemed to be crouching, waiting.

"Okay, that's it! Another day I didn't write anything. Strike two! What's the matter with me, other than being flaky enough to talk to an empty house?"

Tori walked quickly through the large rooms, turning on lights as she did. She knew that from outside, the house looked like someone inside was afraid of the dark.

Refilling her coffee mug, Tori took it to her recliner. Flipping open the TV schedule, she saw there were several sitcoms coming on she hadn't taken time to watch before.

"Big Bang Theory, hmm? I wonder if that's any good. Well, I guess I'm getting ready to find out."

Closing her eyes, she shook her head at her own idiocy.

"And while you're at it, Tori, stop talking to yourself. Maybe I should get a dog, at least then I'd have an excuse for talking out loud."

Tori decided she liked the show "Big Bang Theory" very much. Television, just like most things people take for granted, was a luxury for Tori. She was always too busy writing to watch TV, or live life. Since writing productively was a doubtful prospect, Tori decided she would watch the rest of the comedic line-up.

After that she watched the news, a special on whales, and a movie on her one and only pay channel. She rose out of the recliner to stumble into the computer room, determined to write something, *anything*, so the night wasn't a total loss.

She typed the opening chapter of a book which she felt was all wrong. She typed nonsense words then hit all the symbol keys, just playing around. She tapped the backspace key repeatedly and watched the cursor gobble the words from the screen. The shrill screams of the dying words echoed around her writer's brain and she laughed at herself for having such a silly imagination. When she began to yawn she realized she was putting off going to bed.

The house seems so big lately. What's the matter with me? I'm starting to act like a kid, being afraid of the dark, and the silence, and the sudden noises. This is truly crazy! I'm going to take my shower and go to bed like I always do. Well, I guess I could take my shower in the morning, since it's kinda cold with the draft and all. Okay, I'll take my shower in the morning, but I am going to bed right now. I'm a grown woman and NOT afraid of the boogeyman!

Tori changed into her warm flannel pajamas and started to her bedroom. She paused in the hallway long enough to flip on the light in the bathroom. She stood in front of the half-closed door and stuck out her tongue at the beam of light falling into the hallway.

A puff of wind hit her in the face, strong enough to ruffle her hair and dry the saliva on her outstretched tongue. It lasted only a moment but it left Tori shaking.

What the hell was that? Man, I've got to get someone in here to check this old house for drafts. But, what if it wasn't a draft? What if it was a... and if I start thinking like that I'll be wearing one of those cute little white jackets that buckle in the back. There I'll be, sitting cross-legged in the middle of the room, slobbering all over myself... Oh, shut up, you idiot and go to bed like a big girl! Sheesh! That imagination is going to drive you crazy yet. At least it'd be a short trip and I'd probably get great mileage.

Tori crawled between the sheets. She punched the pillow several times, trying to shape it into an implement of sleep.

For over an hour Tori tossed and turned. Finally falling into a restless slumber, she was treated to a dream so beautiful, and frightening, she would remember it always.

* * *

She was bathing in a sapphire-blue stream, the water cool on her sun-warmed back and up-turned face. Then insidiously, the idyllic setting was being lashed by wind that screamed through the trees at the water's edge. Thunderclouds appeared in seconds and the water began to churn into an alarming whirlpool. Tori was pulled toward the swirling water and she fought to swim toward the mossy bank. Fear wrapped itself around her spine and she was frantic to the point of hysteria. She began to fight even harder.

Her legs were leaden weights, sluggish, reluctant to obey her will to move. *Move damn it!* The torrent of water turned murky as it slipped past her lips and into her mouth opening in a scream. As the brackish water filled her throat the scream was drowned into silence. She could feel herself losing consciousness and gave into the despairing reality of her own death. She grew limp and allowed herself to slip further into a watery grave.

Strong arms pulled her from the water now stilled to a glassy sheen and full lips covered hers. Gently, insistently, life-sustaining air was forced into her quiet lungs. Gasping, spitting vile, fetid water over the ground, Tori coughed back to consciousness. Cool, wet fingers soothed her temple as she sputtered. Loving fingers lifted her trembling chin upward and she stared into the blue eyes she so loved.

* * *

"Avery!"

Still gasping for air, she awoke from the sweat-drenched dream. She sat bolt upright in the middle of the bed, pulling in great lungs of full sweet, blessed oxygen. Tori was crying with disappointment and shaking uncontrollably by after-shocks of a desire never experienced before.

Her tears soon melted into laughter as she finally realized the all-too-real dream was just that—a lovely, frustrating dream.

Damn! I can't fulfill a fantasy, even in my dreams! My life stinks!

Knowing that sleep would not be her companion this night, Tori pulled on her terrycloth robe and walked barefoot to the computer room.

No rest for the weary. Or is it the wicked?

The blackness of the room was awash with bright dancing colors from the monitor's screensaver. For a few moments, Tori stood mesmerized by the changing hues on the screen. She made a conscious effort to shake herself into movement, walking to the keyboard with purpose.

You're awake, you're here, now write! Mr. Big Shot Editor won't be too impressed with a stack of blank pages! You've got the synopsis, now all you have to do is actually write the book. Come on, girl, you've done this before!

Tori fell into the contoured desk chair, ready to disappoint herself once again this night. She just couldn't understand why she was having such a tough time getting in the groove. She leaned back in the chair, head hanging over the backrest.

Again, she allowed her mind to go strolling through fields that covered Avery Norcross' lands. A heavy fog covered the moors and Tori could almost feel the cool mist of it fall on her face. She continued to peer through the density until, at last, she saw him!

Man and horse seemed to be one as they sat atop a rocky ridge rising from the damp earth. Mankala snorted and danced in place, anxious to run. Avery held the large steed at bay despite the way the superb animal tossed his massive head against the reigns until master leaned down to whisper something only Mankala could hear. The beautiful animal calmed, head high, waiting for commands. The ruggedly handsome man appeared to be looking for something, or someone. Tori could almost sense when he found whatever, or whoever, he was looking for.

Avery sat straighter in the saddle. Mankala felt his master's excitement and reacted by rearing up on his back legs. Tori could feel, as well as see, Avery's smile dazzling in the moonlight; her legs grew weak.

Man and horse began to ride slowly, even though Lori sensed that Mankala wanted to race wherever he went. Tori could hear Avery's fierce commands that controlled the equestrian masterpiece. As slowly as they were moving, they still grew closer at an alarming rate. Tori almost felt as if they were traveling in a straight line toward her. Her eyes were opened so wide they watered as she watched their approach.

Mankala was in a playful mood, prancing sideways down the hill. Avery, losing his patience but never his focus, demanded the horse act accordingly. Tori could now see the buckles on Avery's boots and Mankala's warm exhalations in the cold night air. At no point did they deviate from their course, approaching within twenty feet from where Tori felt she stood.

Avery was staring into her eyes, a smoldering look of desire on his face. Mankala nodded his head up and down as if in agreement of his master's emotion. They stopped ten feet from Tori's view. Mankala bent one knee and lowered his sleek head in a bow. Avery, too, removed his hat, and in a sweeping gesture bowed at the waist.

"Good evening, Milady!"

Frantically, Tori's mind whirled around to survey the surrounding countryside, looking for whomever he was speaking to.

"No, lovely lady, there's no one here but you and I. 'Tis you I am speaking to."

Tori's heart raced until it had difficulty keeping up with her torrent of disbelief and fear. Her lungs couldn't expand fast enough and she grew faint. She could feel herself losing the fight to stay conscious, yet she could see Avery extend his hand toward her.

As she slipped away, Tori plainly heard Avery's deep bass voice shouting in alarm.

"No, wait! Please, Victoria! Please..."

Tori nearly fell out of the desk chair as she awoke. Groggy, she regained her balance then stared at the computer monitor. Words covered the screen and she saw in the bottom right corner that she had written twenty pages *while she had been asleep!* Like a frightened little girl, she panted for breath as she rubbed the sleep from her eyes with her fists.

O God! What was that? What just happened? This is too weird, even for my wacky imagination! It all seemed so real. It felt like I could have reached out to touch him. And then to wake up and find I've written twenty pages in my sleep. Whew! I know I said it would be cool to have a ghostwriter but I was only kidding! I just don't get it. But would I even really want the answers if I could have them? Nope, I don't think so! That was some wild dream. Can sleep deprivation actually cause a person to hallucinate? Oh, I really need to get more rest!

Tori ran her fingers through her tangled curls then dropped her hands to smooth the wrinkles of her sleep-rumpled robe. She immediately jerked her hands away from her clothing. She stared incredulously at the moisture on her hands.

Just like condensation from a gently falling mist—or fog!

Tori jumped up, knocking her chair to the floor. She ran from the room, coming to a stop in the kitchen. Her chest was heaving from the exertion of the short run and the disbelieving terror. As she stood there, she tried to regroup her thoughts.

I wonder what is written on the computer. Is it my own words, or someone else's? Should I look? Of course I should! This is preposterous! There is no writing phantom and the words will be mine.

Squaring her shoulders, puffing out her chest, and lifting her head and jaw locked in place, Tori walked back into the computer room. The screen saver had kicked in and she tapped the space bar to stop it. The words flickered into reality and Tori read them with a sense of dread.

But she had no reason to worry. The words were, indeed, hers and the rhythm was perfection. The story line was pure, imaginative, and each line flowed smoothly into the next. Tori was amazed at the train of thought she had chosen but she was also pleased with herself.

This novel, as with the rest of the series, centered on Avery Norcross and his ladylove. However, this one promised to be more lusty, and more loving, than all the others. She read the words out loud, speaking in her own type of cadence, lending sincerity to the words. Yes, she definitely liked it.

Wow! Maybe I should write in my sleep more often! Oh, Lydia's going to love this one!

If at that moment Tori had to think of one word to describe how she felt, it would have been *satisfaction*. It didn't matter that she couldn't remember writing those beautiful words, or even from where she had gotten the idea, her new book had begun. And she felt that it just may be the best she had ever written. She once read an interview with a well-known author who had said that every book he had written had been the best book he had ever done. He continued to say that for a writer to be an accomplished author, he had to feel that each and every book he wrote was the best of his career. Tori hadn't understood this before, but she could now imagine how good it must feel.

She didn't notice the lonely silence of the house that night. Any sounds that normally would scare her were drowned out by her euphoric state of mind. As she gathered her things to take a long, relaxing bath, she hummed one of her all-time favorite songs from 1959. She poured a generous amount of bubble bath under the cascade of hot water. She removed her clothing and dropped them into the wicker basket next to the sink. The bathroom filled with a fragrant vapor as Tori added words to the humming, changing it just a little. Her happiness took control and while she moved her shoulders and feet in some semblance of dance, she clutched an empty cardboard cylinder that had once held toilet tissue, and sang into one end of it.

"Every night, I hope and pray a dream lover will come my way... a man to hold in my arms and know the magic of his charms. Because I want (yeah yeah yeah) a man, (yeah yeah yeah) to call my own… I want a dream lover, so I don't have to dream alone…"

In the hallway outside the bathroom door, Avery Norcross smiled at Tori's off-key singing.

Chapter Four

Tori slept in peace with mind and body resting together in blissful harmony. No dreams, good or bad, and no nerve-jarring surprises to awaken her. At six o'clock she was fully awake, as if she had set an alarm clock the night before. She sat in bed, yawning across the chasm that separates the valleys of sleep and waking. She was trying to remember what had happened the night before to make her feel so happy. When she did, a smile covered her relaxed features. Mother Nature was calling, but before Tori could get to the bathroom the telephone rang.

"Good morning!"

"Tori? How can you sound so chipper when someone wakes you from a dead sleep?"

Laughing, Tori sat back down on the bed, crossing her legs against the urge.

"Lydia? What in the world are you doing out of bed so early?"

Lydia's throaty laugh vibrated through the receiver.

"Who said I was out of bed?"

"Okay, why are you awake at this time of the morning?"

"I've not been to sleep, yet."

Tori was puzzled. Was something wrong?

Lydia lowered her voice and whispered into the phone.

"I've been busy."

"All night? What've you been doing that's so important you can't sleep?"

"Just buzzing around, you know, like a busy little bee."

"A bee? Why are you talking in code? My brain isn't fully awake yet and you want me to solve a puzzle?"

Even through the telephone, Tori could hear the exasperation in Lydia's voice.

"Think about it, darling, and you'll know what I'm talking about."

Tori thoughtfully stared into space, trying to figure out what her insane agent was trying to tell her. By now, she was swinging her crossed legs, impatient to finish this conversation.

Bee. Buzzing? A buzzing bee? B? B.E.E.? Oh, B.E.! If that isn't it, I'm hanging up! I gotta pee so bad!

"Well, Lydia, either you're in a Bachelor of Engineering program, or you're with Big Shot Editor."

"Ta-da! I knew my brilliant little writer could solve the mystery."

"Look, Lydia, I'm real happy one of us got lucky, even if it wasn't me. But I have to run, literally. I've got more water backed up than Hoover Dam. So, if you'll excuse me..."

"Really, Victoria, you don't have to be so crass..."

Click! Tori dropped the receiver into its cradle as she rushed from the room.

* * *

Tori prepared a huge breakfast for herself. She wolfed down two eggs, bacon, toast, a muffin, and a large glass of milk. She was shocked at herself for eating so much, even as she was undoing the top button of her jeans.

As her food digested, Tori thought about what she would do that morning. The responsible thing to do would be work on her book, but she didn't feel like being responsible right now.

I know; I'll go shopping! Yeah! I'm going to buy a dress. A dress, you say? But you only wear dresses under protest. Well, I'm a woman and I can change my mind. That's my prerogative. My inalienable right under the Southern Belle Constitution! And it's going to be a right purty one, too!

Giggling, Tori jumped up from her seat to plug in the old hot rollers. If she was going to buy a dress, she ought to curl her hair. She didn't know why that made sense, but it did, at least to her. Not even barking her shin on the table leg altered her light mood.

The weather was as happy as Tori's feelings. The sun had at last awoken to chase the chill from the late fall day. Leaves playfully danced around her feet in a swirling eddy, looking for a playmate.

Tori's first stop was a dress boutique. The name of the store, Remembrance, was painted in an old world-style script. If she had stopped to think this over, she would have remembered that she had never been in a boutique in her life. In fact, just the word *boutique* used to irritate her to no end, but nothing could irritate Tori today.

In the back of the shop was a display of Victorian-style clothing. Yards and yards of various colors of velvet, and rows of tiny buttons that would require the patience of Job to fasten. This is where Tori was drawn, as a magnet to steel. She held each dress, running the smooth material between her fingers, and "oohed" and "ahhed", appreciatively. She had seen other women behave the same way and it had always annoyed her. But for some strange reason Tori was, herself, acting quite differently on this glorious morning.

One dress in particular grabbed her attention. Floor-length, with what seemed to be a million mock-seed pearl buttons down the back, the emerald green dress with a plunging neckline beckoned her. She lifted it from the rack and held it in front of her. The skirt front of the dress had been sewn open to give a tantalizing view of yards of delicate lace beneath. She walked to a mirror, and holding out the side of the full skirt, swayed in front of her reflection, loving the way the material flowed.

The salesclerk knew a sale when she saw one.

"That would look stunning on you, Miss. Will you be trying it on?"

Blushing at being caught acting like a fool, Tori shook her head.

"Uh, no, thank you. I'm really just browsing."

Feeling her commission slipping through her fingers, the saleslady hastened to assure Tori that the dress was made for her.

"Really, Miss, you would look gorgeous in this!"

"Oh, I just don't know. Why would I want a formal velvet gown? I'm afraid I would look ridiculous in it."

"No! The color would be perfect with your lovely red hair. Please, just try it on. You'll fall in love with it when you see how beautiful you look."

Tori looked at the price tag hanging from the sleeve and felt faint.

O God! I'd have to sell a lot of books to pay for this dress.

"No, I'm sorry. I like the dress, but I simply can't afford it, even if I did have somewhere to wear it."

The salesclerk's face fell, and she turned away.

As Tori was walking toward the door, head held low, her eye caught the gleam of one particular ring resting in a jewelry display case. The smile that met her request to see the ring closer made Tori uncomfortable, as if the ring was already a commission for the salesclerk.

The saleslady recognized Tori's curiosity and hurried to open the display case as Tori nodded her approval of that particular ring.

Tori delicately turned the ring around in the palm of her hand, admiring the design. The gold was inundated with tiny green symbols, though too small to appreciate with the naked eye. The woman behind the counter, as if reading her mind, handed Tori a magnifying glass.

As the symbols focused, Tori gasped and knew at once that she had to buy it, no matter what the cost. In old English lettering, she read

My Victoria—My love

A giddy, schoolgirl feeling rushed over her and Tori knew, at that moment, that she was going to buy the ring. The small price tag suspended from the ring caused only a moment's hesitation.

Damn the price!

"Miss, you want to try it on?"

"Never mind; it doesn't matter if it fits or not, I like it and I'm buying it. Not only that, but I'm buying that gorgeous jade green dress to match the ring. How does that sound to you?"

The salesclerk's face became wreathed in a smile, mentally adding her percentage of the sale to her paycheck."

"I think that sounds splendid! I like a woman who knows her mind. Will that be cash or charge?"

Even though she intended to have the items, Tori still swallowed hard when she wrote the check.

Clutching the shop bag in her hand, Tori rushed to her car and stowed the impulsive purchases in the car trunk. All desire to shop had dissipated, so Tori went home.

Once inside the house, she opened a small drawer of her jewelry box. She took out the rest of the items there and a few gave her sentimental twinges at the memories they stirred. She slid the box containing the ring to the back of the drawer and put the rest of the jewelry over it. The dress she placed in a garment bag and hung at the end of the rod in her closet.

This is silly. Good grief! I act like I'm hiding those things! Who am I hiding them from? Myself? I don't even know why I bought them! And the money I just threw away! Omigod, I must be losing my mind!

The shrill summon of the telephone startled her, jolting Tori out her self-recrimination.

"Hello?"

"Good afternoon, sweetheart."

"Mom! How are you?"

"I'm fine, dear. I called earlier but there was no answer."

"Well, Mom, that's probably because no one was home."

Sharon laughed good-naturedly.

"Don't be such a smart-mouth, Victoria Lynn!"

"Uh oh. Whenever I hear first and middle name, I know I'm skating on thin ice."

"That's right."

"Okay, Mommy dearest, I'm sorry. You must have called while I was out shopping."

"Shopping? You, Tori? You actually went out, all by yourself, with no pressure and shopped? Are you ill?"

Tori exhaled the sigh that all daughters reserve for when their mothers are insufferably correct.

"Yeah. I do that, sometimes."

"Since when, Tori? Lydia and I beg you to go with us every time we go shopping. The few times you have conceded to join us, it was obvious you were bored to tears and only wanted to go home. Anyway, never mind all that. What did you buy?"

"Oh, nothing. I was just looking."

"Looking? For what?"

Tori hesitated, uncharacteristically annoyed with her mother's prying.

"Books. I was looking at books—for research."

"Oh, for heaven's sake, Tori. Don't you have enough books? Why don't you buy a pretty dress? Oh, I forgot. You don't like dresses, do you? I wish you did, because you look so pretty, so *feminine*, whenever you're forced to wear one."

"Yeah, right," Tori sighed. "I'm sorry if I just feel more comfortable in jeans and a big, ol' sloppy t-shirt. Do I disappoint you, Mom?"

"No, of course not, darling. I would be proud of you if you wore a burlap sack with a rope for a belt. My baby is lovely, no matter what she wears. If intelligence and love could be worn outside, you would be even more beautiful, the loveliest woman this world has ever seen."

"Aw, shucks, Ma'am! You're embarrassing me. You might be happy to know that I did something totally frivolous; I did actually buy a ring. Surprise!"

"You're right, Tori, that does make me happy. Tell me what it looks like."

She didn't know why, but Tori didn't mention the dress.

"Aw, the ring's nothing special, just a gold-plated band with some kind of cheap green glass around it. I'll show you sometime. What're you and your partner in crime up to today?" Sharon would make such a fuss if she knew not only how beautiful, antique and expensive the ring was, but she'd probably tell Lydia. Tori wasn't in the mood for a lecture.

"Well, that's one reason I'm calling. Lydia thought we girls might enjoy having dinner together, then catch a movie after. It sounds like a good idea to me. What d'you think? Want to go? Come on, honey. Spend some time with your two biggest fans."

Tori surprised her mother by saying yes. She felt guilty when she heard the gratitude in Sharon's voice. She was going to have to spend more time with her mother and stop locking herself in the computer room for weeks at a time. Living alone, being your own boss, made it easy to forget about family that missed and loved you.

They discussed meeting Lydia at the restaurant at seven o'clock. Then they talked about what movies were available.

"Wear something warm tonight, Tori. It's supposed to be quite chilly."

"Yes, Mommy."

"There goes that mouth, again! See you at seven, honey. I love you."

"I love you too, Mom."

Tori sat down in front of the computer to knock out a few more pages before she had to leave for dinner. She lost track of time and was shocked when she looked at the clock and saw it was already six o'clock. Later, she wasn't sure if she had become immersed in her writing or if she had fallen asleep again.

It was right after dessert that Tori discovered the *real* reason for her dinner invitation. Mother and agent had decided it was high time Tori started dating. They even had a couple of prospects lined up. When Tori saw where the conversation was leading, she began to shake her head, more forcefully with each sentence spoken.

"No, no, no! I do *not* need a date. Where is it written that I *have* to be with a man to be happy and fulfilled? Neither one of you is married, yet you seem to be relatively happy."

Lydia broke in before Sharon could open her mouth, as usual.

"No, love, neither one of us is married. But we do date, and would get married in a heartbeat, if the right man came along. At least we're trying and not moldering away at home just sitting on our arse."

Tori covered her mouth to stifle the laughter bubbling up.

"Arse? You know, it's funny, Lydia, that whenever you're angry, or drunk, your cockney accent just slips out. And all that money you spent for accent adjustment!"

Lydia's face was turning a bright red as she glanced around the restaurant, as if to remind herself she was in public.

"Just don't you worry about my accent, young lady. Sharon, didn't you teach this brat to watch her manners?"

Tori's grin widened.

"Yes, and she also taught me to respect my elders. I'm sorry if I haven't shown you the respect your age deserves, Lydia."

Lydia saw the comment for what it was, her young client teasing her.

"Why I oughta..."

Sharon hadn't spoken for several minutes because she was overcome with trying to hold the laughter inside. Unable to hold it any longer, she exploded, causing all heads in the restaurant to turn. Gaining control of herself, she turned to her dinner companions.

"Maybe we should get out of here before we're thrown out. It's about time for the movie, anyway."

The three ladies walked out, drawing appreciative glances from the male patrons. Most of the women present began to prattle about proper conduct in public.

The movie, about a young warrior of the eighteenth century, was incredibly romantic. Tori was so enthralled, so intensely concentrated on the film, she scarcely breathed until the final credits rolled over the screen. She turned to Lydia and Sharon and was touched when she noticed they had been crying. Both women dabbed at their eyes, glancing at Tori as if daring her to comment on it. Few words were spoken as they each walked to their car. A warm glow of a shared experience enveloped them as they kissed each other good night.

Tori didn't bother to turn on the car radio. She drove home wrapped in a filmy haze that only the romantic at heart could understand. The landscape passed without notice and Tori later didn't remember the whole trip home.

The hush of the house welcomed Tori like an old friend. She closed the door behind her, dropped her purse and removed her jacket, all without conscious effort. There was a shiny patina over her face and an unfocused look in her eyes. It softened her mouth and gave the appearance of a woman whose long-suppressed desires were fighting to overcome her control.

Tori turned on the bath water, steam rising to blur her image in the wide expanse of mirror over the sink. She leaned against the doorframe, staring into the damp mist, and wearing a soft smile. In her mind, Tori was imagining Avery Norcross in the lead of the movie she had just seen. The proud horse he rode was Mankala, man and beast roaming the countryside. The leading lady in the film was her, a role she would have clasped to her heart.

She and Avery were lying beneath an outcropping of rock, which formed a cave for the lovers to meet in secret. He whispered words of love in her eager ear and held her in his lover's embrace. Mankala stood watch over his master and his woman, raising his head occasionally to survey the land, just as his master did. Avery kissed her softly, tenderly removing the green velvet dress from her trembling body. Her back arched in acceptance and desire...

And water poured over the edge of the tub to soak the carpet.

"Oh man! Stand here daydreaming like a sex-starved fool and ruining the floor! I shouldn't let my imagination take over unless I'm in the safety of the computer room. God, what a mess!"

It took every towel she owned to damp dry the mess. She threw all of them in the washer then went to take her bath. Annoyance evaporated as she worked shampoo through her long hair. Artificial light cast shimmering glints across the copper curls. Tori leaned back to allow the warm water to ease aching muscles and she fell into a deep sleep, almost immediately.

An arctic blast of air touched her body, causing the flesh to pucker in reaction to the drop in temperature. Tori jumped from the tub, pulling the plug as she stood on the damp carpet. Feeling as if someone were watching her, she spun around to grab her towel. But, of course, there was no one there.

Looking around the bathroom, and seeing nothing out of the ordinary, Tori, nevertheless, shut the door. She knew it was a silly thing to do, since there was no one in the house but herself. She just felt more secure with the black hallway being shielded from view.

Preparations for bed became more frenzied as Tori wanted to just get out of the bathroom to search the rest of the house. Rationally, she knew there was no one else there and nothing to harm her. Psychically, she was beginning to feel as if she wasn't alone.

Pulling her bathrobe over her wet body, Tori opened the door cautiously. Droplets of water made a spattering noise on the varnished floor of the hall as she peered into the darkness. She heard a moan that rooted her to the floor, until she realized she was the one making the sound.

O God, why didn't I leave the lights on?

Taking a deep breath, Tori raced to the end of the hall, slamming her hand against the light switch. Instantly, the hall and part of the living room were bathed in welcoming light. Feeling a little braver with illumination, Tori rushed through the house, turning on all the lights. Only then did she take time to search each room completely, with her largest butcher knife in her hand, held behind her back so she could use the element of surprise against an invader.

Deciding that, indeed, the house was empty, Tori dropped the knife back into the kitchen drawer. She leaned against the cool tile of the counter top and laughed at herself. One of those movies that had scared her so badly a few years before flashed through her mind. She recalled how a psychic had been called to rid a house, and its occupants, of a mean-spirited ghost. Smoothing her hair back in imitation of the small-statured woman from the movie, Tori made a declaration to herself.

"This house is clean."

She forced herself to extinguish the light in the kitchen, but allowed herself the luxury of leaving every other light burning. She hurriedly dried her hair, just knowing that the blow dryer was covering up the sound of someone sneaking up on her. She brushed her teeth as she stared in the mirror for the shape of a man coming into the room. Her nerves were twitching and adrenaline pulsed through her veins, causing her heart to race.

I can't go to sleep when I can feel the blood pounding in my ears. I wonder if I still have one of those sleeping pills Mom insisted the doctor give me after my divorce.

Opening the medicine cabinet, Tori found the bottle of prescription drugs next to the aspirin. Her hands were shaking as she struggled to open it. Dropping one into her hand, she got a drink of water; the glass chattering against her teeth as she swallowed. Setting the glass back down on the porcelain sink, gently, she felt as if she had escaped the bathroom, rather than simply just leaving it.

Tori sat in her chair, picked up the remote control and started flipping through the channels. One of the local stations was showing an all-night special on the artists of Motown. Tori pulled her throw blanket over her legs and sank into the cushions of the chair in contentment.

Within minutes she realized she wasn't going to be able to stay awake, which was fine with her. She turned up the television volume and folded the blanket over the chair arm. Staggering, she eventually made it to her bedroom, where she collapsed on top of the cover.

When she was deeply asleep, the blanket was lifted to cover her shivering body. The right side of the bed showed no depression where Avery lay beside Tori. He was turned on his side so he could stare into her face.

He lovingly caressed her cheek, and in her sleep, Tori unknowingly smiled at the feather-light touch of her own creation.

Chapter Five

Tori was jolted awake by bitter cold hitting her face. Sunlight poured into the bedroom window but it did little to heat the room. She stood, pulling the blanket with her, and wrapped it around her shoulders. She shuffled into the hallway and peered at the thermostat with sleep-puffy eyes.

"Oh, now, that's just marvelous! The stupid furnace isn't working and it's only fifty degrees in here. No wonder I'm shivering."

Her feet became entangled in the blanket several times as she was trying to pry the door loose from the furnace. Once she had it free, she dropped the metal covering to the floor where it landed with a tinny clang. Her knee joints popped in the quiet house as Tori knelt to check the pilot light.

"Yeah, sure. I knew it, I just knew it! I hate it when this happens and I have to risk life and limb to relight it. I'm gonna blow myself up someday just trying to stay warm. Where the heck did I put those long kitchen matches?"

Stumbling through the house, the blanket was now more of a nuisance than a warm friend. Irritation followed the course of the comforter as Tori threw it across the room.

She looked in every logical place she could think of, and a few illogical ones, as well, but couldn't find the matches. She was exasperated to the point of tears when she heard the familiar *whoosh!* of the furnace kicking in.

Ah, now, that's impossible! The pilot light was off, I saw it myself; not working. A furnace does not relight itself. Or can it? Maybe I had better call a repairman. I don't want the thing to explode while I'm asleep less than fifteen feet away! Man, oh man, this is just too weird!

Right on the heels of this came yet another irritating revelation.

God, I've got one hell of a headache! That sleeping pill was just a cheap excuse for a hangover. Whew! No more of those dastardly little devils. Now, where's my aspirin? I think I need about twenty of them!

The ring of the telephone sliced through her head like a knife—a dull knife. The pain and annoyance was etched clearly on her puffy face.

"What is it with these people? Don't they ever sleep? I have one agent, and one mother, and they both get up with the chickens!"

Snatching the phone and banging her forehead in the process did little to temper Tori's foul mood.

"Yeah?"

Sharon's usually sunny voice sounded confused, and unsure.

"Tori? Are you okay?"

"Yes, Mom. Why shouldn't I be?"

"Well, it's silly, I know, but I had a terrible nightmare about you last night. I've been up for hours, just waiting until I thought it was late enough to call you. I'm sorry, honey. I hope I didn't wake you. I was just worried..."

Instantly sorry for her curt response to her mother's concern, Tori quickly apologized.

"Oh, Mom, I'm sorry. No, you didn't wake me. I took one of those sleeping pills the doctor gave me and woke up feeling wiped out. And when I got out of bed, I walked into a freezer. The pilot light was out on the furnace."

"Tori, honey, come over here. We'll call a repairman. While you're waiting for him, I'll fix you breakfast."

"No, that's sweet of you, Mom, but I'm fine. For some weird reason the heat came back on, all by itself."

"Tori, that's not possible, dear."

"I know that, and you know that, but evidently the furnace doesn't know that. Anywho, that's what happened. The temperature's already up to sixty-five, and climbing. I appreciate the offer, but I think I'll just hang out here today and get some writing done."

"Alright, dear, if you're sure. As long as I know you're okay, I'll stop worrying. I know you're a grown woman, Tori, but to me, you'll always be my little girl. I guess I get a little silly sometimes."

Knowing her mother wanted to be reassured, Tori obliged her.

"No, you're not silly, Mom. And I would be hurt if you ever quit worrying about me. I count on it. It means a lot to know that I'll always have someone who loves me, no matter how grouchy, or crazy, I get. I love you, Mom."

"I love you, too, sweet Tori. Good bye, honey."

"Good bye, Mom."

Let me see, it's only seven o'clock in the morning and I've already hurt the sweetest woman in the world! For an encore, maybe I can get in my car and run over a few innocent kids on their way to school! I'm really a piece of...

The thought was never completed. Behind her, Tori heard what sounded like a hand, a very heavy hand, being slammed down on the kitchen counter. It was an expression of anger.

Not bothering to dress, Tori grabbed her clothes, shoes, and purse, and ran to her car. Her hands were trembling so badly that she had difficulty putting the key in the ignition. Once she got the car started, *finally!, finally!, ohthankyouGod!,* she pulled away from the house, tires squealing. But she ran over no children on their way to school.

She pulled into her mother's driveway, for once reaching the door before Sharon could get there. Her whole body was shaking and her mother made a worried exclamation when she saw her daughter's face.

"Oh, honey, what's wrong? Hurry up; get in the house. Do you want a cup of coffee? You look like you've seen a ghost!"

There was no humor in Tori's dry laughter.

"Well, Mom, I didn't actually *see* a ghost, but I'm pretty sure there's one in my house!"

Sharon spun around in her small, but efficient, kitchen. Her expression was of complete, and utter, disbelief.

"Tori! You can't possibly really mean that! Honey, you know there's no such thing as ghosts. It's just your wonderful, but all too vivid, imagination, darling."

Staring into her mother's eyes, Tori began to slowly shake her head.

"I don't know anymore, Mom. There have been some... how should I say this? I've had a few strange things happen to me in that house. I may be a writer, and I'll admit my imagination gets pretty wild, but not even I could imagine this!"

Sharon put the cup of steaming coffee on the bar in front of Tori. Her own hand was shaking. She didn't know what was going on, but she knew she was worried about her child.

"Tell me about it, Sweetheart. All of it, and hold nothing back."

Tori put her hand over her mother's, a gesture of reassurance.

"I'm really not crazy, you know."

"No, of course not, honey."

"Well, you're wearing your 'my daughter's a raving lunatic' face. If I tell you, it will only scare you more. Maybe this is something I have to work out for myself, Mom."

A look of stern disapproval marred Sharon's lovely face and Tori almost giggled at her mother's intensity. If she hadn't been so frightened, this whole thing might have been funny. But it wasn't; it was scary.

Tori thought about just leaving, not bothering her mother with tales of ghosts and ghouls. But she was afraid that, despite her mother's age, she would field-tackle Tori before she reached the door. Now, that was funny. The visual image of Sharon jumping her made Tori, in spite of what had happened, laugh out loud.

"What's so funny, Tori? You are one strange kid. Practically hysterical one minute, and laughing the next. Hmmm, I wonder if you're mentally sound."

"Hey, hey, hey! I came here for emotional support and you're making fun of me. What kind of mother are you, anyway?"

"Emotional support? I'd think you need emotional therapy! Aw, come on, Tori, lighten up, will ya? I'm only trying to cheer you up."

"By insulting me? Listen to me! Of course that's what you're doing. That's the way we've always done it, right? It's just that, sometimes, our insulting type of humor gets on my nerves."

Sharon walked around the counter and put her arms around her only child. She urged Tori to move, by gently pressing against her shoulders.

"Let's go in the living room where it's more comfortable. We'll drink our coffee and you're going to tell dear old Mom what's been going on in your house."

They talked for over two hours. Tori would relate an experience with her "ghost" and Sharon would answer with a logical explanation. Both women were getting annoyed with the other one for not seeing things in their proper light.

The end result of their long conversation was to go back and visit the scene of the crime. Each woman was smugly certain the other one would be proven wrong. Sharon believed she could convince her daughter that there were reasons for each oddity and Tori just knew her mother was an unbelieving ninny.

The house was suffocating. The thermostat that Tori had turned up now registered eighty degrees; they started shedding clothes as they walked.

The first room they inspected was the kitchen. Tori was about to explain the slamming sound that had driven her from the house when her mother snorted.

"Could this be what you heard, dear?" She held up a very large, heavy cookbook that was lying face down on the counter. Tori had gotten it when she was into her "I want to learn how to cook" phase. The book had been standing on the microwave oven since the first day it came into the house.

"I didn't see that earlier! How did it get there?"

"I think that you were so busy getting out of here that you didn't stop to look, Tori."

"But, why would it fall? It's been on the microwave for... I don't know how long. Why would it, all of a sudden, just fly off?"

"I really don't think it flew anywhere. An old house settles, Tori, and everything in the house shifts when it does. That book's probably been on the verge of sliding off for a long time. One final shift, or the movement of your step, and wham! There it goes."

"Well, what about all the other stuff, Mom? What's your rational explanation for those?"

Sharon hugged her daughter to her, and kissed her forehead.

"But, Mom, what about the cold wind on my face waking me?"

"Well, the furnace *was* off at the time."

"Okay, what about feeling someone standing behind me, in the computer room?"

"Your imagination. Everything that's happened to you can either be explained, or you imagined it."

"Humph! Not everything in this world can be explained, Mom."

"If it is in this world, Tori, it most certainly *can* be explained. If it isn't in this world, well, that's a different story. I'll admit that there are many things in this universe that I can't explain, and neither can anyone else, at least not to my satisfaction."

Tori was somewhat pacified by her mother's admission that there were oddities with no rational answer. But that didn't stop her from being scared. All the logic in the world would only go so far and then pure terror could set in. But, for the moment, Tori was more than happy to accept Sharon's theories. She didn't *want* to believe there was something strange in her home.

Maybe it truly was her cursed, over-active imagination. Even as a child, Tori had always enjoyed being melodramatic. Could this be an example of believing her own hype? If so, she needed to make that call to a therapist-soon!

What Tori didn't know, couldn't know, was that the events that had happened were far from logical. There definitely was a presence in her house. It wasn't a monster, and it wasn't exactly a ghost. It was a being with form, but no substance. It was a being that was growing stronger with each day. It was a being that was angry with Tori when she degraded herself, or her capabilities. It was an entity that wanted to be physically near Tori, and was getting closer to that desire with each passing day.

Chapter Six

...her hand trembled as she reached out to trace the outline of his provocative mouth. He took her hand and brought the palm to his lips, softly kissing it, and she felt his breath waltz along her wrist.

He laid her upon the fragrant grass, then encircled her body with his strong arms. He nuzzled her neck, reaching out his tongue to trail sweet fire along her shoulder. He lowered his face, softly nipping at the warm hollow of the valley...

The concentrated frown deepened between her eyes. Tori sighed, then snatched the phone from its cradle, still focused on the computer monitor and the sensual words waiting there.

"Um... yes?"

"Tori? Hi, it's Jim."

Four simple, innocent words that tightened her chest, and made her lose all concentration on what Avery was about to do next. This was a voice she hadn't heard in over a year.

"Jim! Hello! How are you?"

"Well... Actually, I'm doing great. Things are going so well in my life; I couldn't stand it if it were any better."

Her fingers twisted the phone cord into knots, nearly tugging the phone off the desk. Her pale complexion reflected back to her from the computer screen.

"Wow. That's really good to hear, Jim. I'm happy for you. Has something happened to bring about this wonderful change?"

Momentary silence met her question. Tori couldn't understand how Jim could be so happy, yet so reticent to talk about it. She was just about to change the subject when she heard him take a deep breath.

"Tori, I'm getting married."

It was now her turn to be speechless. A hundred thoughts flitted through her mind, burrowing themselves into her heart. She was angry with herself to realize a tear had slid down her cheek.

"That's fantastic! Congratulations. Anyone I know? When's the wedding?"

"No, no, you don't know her. She just moved into the area about a year ago. She's a nurse, working at one of the hospitals here in town."

"A nurse, huh? I'll bet that's interesting. So, you're getting married when?"

"Uh... well... next week."

"Gosh! Next week, huh? Have you been thinking of a big church wedding?"

"No. We're just going to Eureka Springs, Arkansas and find a chapel. We're not worried about a big, splashy affair. We've been living together for a few months, so this is really just a formality. We were going to wait a while longer, but felt it best to do it now."

"But, why? If you've been together all this time, why not just wait and let her have a nice church wedding? Surely she'll want that. What's the hurry?"

Another long stretch of heavy silence, at last broken with his monotone answer, as if he were striving to make his voice noncommittal, devoid of any happiness.

"Well, Shawna's pregnant. She's due in about seven months. We thought it was a good idea to go ahead and make it legal and maybe have a fancy church affair sometime after the baby is born. You know, maybe on our fifth wedding anniversary, or our tenth."

Tori no longer tried to control the silent tears running down her face, but she did wipe at them angrily. As she stared out the window, she thought how ironic it was that the reason she was divorced was the very reason Jim was now remarrying. An uncharacteristic feeling of hatred washed over her, and she knew it was jealousy, with a liberal dose of pain at the knowledge she would never be picking out infant clothing and furniture with Jim, or any other man.

"Well, Jim, congratulations, again. I wish you and your new bride the best of luck. I have to go now. I have something boiling over on the stove. Goodbye."

"Tori! Wait! I didn't mean to upset you. I only thought it fair to tell you before..."

She waited a minute to be sure the connection was broken, then lifted the telephone and placed it on the desk. She didn't think Jim would call back, but she didn't want to talk to him, or anyone else, at the moment.

She laid her head on her crossed arms resting on the edge of the desk. Hot, bitter tears fell onto her lap. She raised her head, picking up a reference book, and savagely threw it across the small room.

And though he was unseen, and the flying object could not yet harm his vaporous form, Avery jerked his body to the side, instinctively dodging the thick book.

* * *

Tori lifted her sleep-drowsy eyes to stare at the wall as she again heard someone knocking at her front door. She glanced at the clock above her computer and realized she'd been out of it again. After Jim's call, she'd evidently cried herself to sleep while leaning over the keyboard. Her headache had not abated. In fact, it seemed to have increased in intensity. Cursing beneath her breath, she stood stiffly to her feet, proving her body complained at the idea of her sleeping at her desk. She shuffled to the door and opened it just few inches until she saw who was standing there.

Sharon's face was pale and her eyes were large in her pretty face.

"Tori? What's wrong? I've been calling you for over two hours and the line was busy. I've been worried to death. Honey, what's going on?"

Behind her mother's back, Tori rubbed her eyes, which felt inflamed and gritty. She took a deep, calming breath as she turned to put her arms around Sharon. She could feel her mother's body held rigid, and the fast, short breaths she was taking.

"Mom, I'm all right. I'm sorry. It seems I have to keep reassuring you, don't I? I suppose I worry you a lot, but I'm a big girl and can take care of myself. I simply took the phone off the hook so I could get some writing done."

Sharon stared into Tori's eyes and disbelief was clearly written in her face.

"Victoria, you've never done that before. And you look as if you've been crying. Honey, please tell me the truth."

Tori fell onto the sofa cushions, leaning her throbbing head against the upholstered arm. Sharon came to sit beside her daughter, taking Tori's cold hand into her own.

"Mom, I've just got this terrible headache I can't seem to shake. I was trying to get some work done and must've fallen asleep at my desk."

"Sweetheart, there's more to this story."

"Okay, you're right. I got a phone call-from Jim"

Sharon's face reddened into a mother's protective shade of concern.

"Oh, really? And what did dear ol' Jim want to discuss with you?"

Tori rubbed her tired face and began to tremble. Sharon's heart squeezed with love for her child.

"Jim just called, Mom, to tell me that he's getting married."

Sharon's gasp of surprise seemed to lend credence to Tori's feeling of betrayal, validating her need to mourn.

"Not only did he tell me he's getting married, but Shawna, his fiancée, is pregnant."

Tori felt herself being pulled into her mother's warm embrace. It was the only thing needed for her to fully give into the hurt that seemed to be tearing her heart apart. She laid her head on her mother's shoulder, her face buried into her neck as when she was a child, and sobbed. Her slender shoulders shook with the passion of her pain.

Spent at last, Tori was comforted by her mother stroking her hair, rubbing her back, murmuring loving words of consolation against her child's tear-streaked cheeks.

Hiccupping, Tori drew away from Sharon to reach for the box of tissues next to the sofa. She loudly blew her red nose, eliciting a grin from her mother. Tori saw her expression and began to giggle. No matter that it was the nearly manic sound sometimes accompanying grief; it still felt good to stop crying.

Sharon joined in the laughter, then stood and pulled Tori to her feet.

"Now, show me that ring you bought—which I'm still in shock about. This has got to be some ring."

Even though she didn't understand it, wariness seeped into Tori's mind at the thought of showing the gold and jade ring to her mother. She didn't realize that a look of secretiveness stole over her puffy face. She was as easy to read as one of her own books.

"Oh, I took it back to the boutique. It was much too expensive, even though it was so not worth it, and I'd never go anywhere to wear it. It was one of those spur-of-the-moment purchases we've all made, then regretted. You know, 'buyer's remorse'. My checking account looks much healthier since I returned it."

She sensed that Sharon didn't believe her and held her breath until her mother's next words proved she wasn't going to push the issue.

"Well, okay, Honey. How about me making us some coffee? That may actually help your headache. Have you taken any aspirin yet? I have some extra-strength ones in my purse. Here, take a couple of these, Tori."

Tori swallowed the pills with her coffee as she listened to Sharon talk about Lydia's details of her night spent with the editor. Sharon laughed out loud at some of the things her best friend had told her, and it felt good to Tori to share in her mother's anecdotes.

After her mother was reassured enough to leave, Tori allowed herself to dwell on the morose feelings she was experiencing. She was at long last permitting herself the luxury of truly mourning the death of a love that she had believed would be forever. Even though it had been five years coming, she was only now grieving.

Along with the dissolution of the marriage, she mourned the loss of a dream never realized. With this she admitted unmitigated anger that it was Shawna, and not she, who would be having Jim's child. Anger at her barrenness filled her heart and hot, scalding tears once again flowed down her face. Tori felt betrayed by her ex-husband going on with his life, fathering a child, being *happy*. She railed against the injustices of life as she stood in the middle of her bedroom, staring at the far wall which still held a portrait taken of her and Jim in happier times.

Tori walked over and took the photograph from the wall. With a calmness that bordered on catatonia, she shuffled into the kitchen and dropped the frame into the garbage. The sound of breaking glass snapped her to attention and she sank to the floor, her arms splayed outward in supplication, her harsh sobs filling the solemn house.

When the sobbing became merely loud sniffles, Tori lifted herself from the floor and shuffled into the bathroom. Opening the mirrored door of the medicine cabinet, she shook two of the sleeping pills into her trembling hand. She stared at the pale, tired face that stared back at her, gulped the pills, then went to the bedroom. She fell across her bed, the crying no longer abrasive, more like silent admissions of failure. She lay on her back, the tears soaking her hair as they fell unabated till the moment she fell asleep.

* * *

Tears coursing down his own face, Avery stretched out his arms as if to hold Tori, to comfort the love of his life. Cursed was this flimsy, nonexistent form he was imprisoned in, unable to hold her, kiss her, show her how truly loved she was. He lifted his head, imploring any God that may take pity on his plight, to give him substance so that he might touch this angel who needed him as much as he needed her. As if in answer to his plea, he could feel a change beginning to take place.

Chapter Seven

Sharon passed Lydia a cup of tea, the aromatic blend wafting through the room to lend a certain coziness to the scene. Sharon's expressive face, much like her own daughter's, belied the fact that something troubled her. The perpetual smile had slipped just a notch, and her pretty lips were a pencil-line in her lovely face.

"Okay, Luv, tell me what's wrong."

Sharon smiled ruefully and tilted her head to one side as she shrugged her shoulders. Surprisingly, a solitary tear gently fell from her blue eyes.

"Lydia, I'm not exactly sure what's wrong. Oh, I have an idea. I do know one thing that has happened, but not the whole story..."

With assumed patience, Lydia placed her cup and saucer on the polished mahogany coffee table.

"I've an idea, Sharon. Instead of you talking in circles and confusing me more, why don't you just lay your cards out for me? How can I play the game if I can't see your hand?"

Sharon chuckled, "Ah, dear Lydia. You always do want me to cut to the chase, don't you, dear?"

"Well, it would make it much easier to help if I knew the rules of the game."

"I'm concerned about Tori, but I don't know that you can help, Lydia. I don't know if anyone can."

"Yes, well, you're still being quite vague, Sharon. Do be a dear and tell me what is going on."

"Lydia, have you noticed how haggard Tori is looking lately? She looks like she never sleeps. I know she's always been somewhat of a recluse, but it seems as if she's withdrawing more and more lately, even from me. Several times her telephone is off the hook, or she simply doesn't answer it. When I can't stand it anymore, I go to her house to find her a wreck, crying or complaining with a terrible headache. Then she tells me that Jim called her to tell her he's getting married, and the woman is pregnant. I'm very worried what this may do to Tori."

"Sweetheart, Tori is a grown woman. The biggest problem I see with adult children is you can't make them listen to you, as if you could when they were younger. Yes, I've noticed the changes in Tori, but she'll be okay. She's much tougher and more resilient than you give her credit for, my dear. Tori may have had the wind knocked out of her, but she'll catch her breath, I just know it."

"I sure hope you're right. It hurts me to see her like this, especially when it seems there's nothing I can do to help her."

"Sharon, I just had a splendid idea! What about us finding her a date?"

"She would probably kill us both. You know she doesn't date. She hasn't dated since the divorce."

Lydia grinned, "Then it's way past time she went out with a nice man, isn't it? I know just the guy, too. He's a writer, so they automatically have something in common. I admit, he writes science-fiction, but a writer nevertheless, right?"

"Oh, I don't know about this, Lydia. Tori is so funny about things like that. I'm sure she will get mad at us if we set her up with this guy."

"Well, alright, but it's a shame. He's close to her age, exquisitely handsome, and has just loads of money."

Sharon's face shined. "Oh, he's wealthy, you say? Tell me, wherever did you meet him?"

Lydia's deep-throated chuckle made Sharon grin.

"He happens to be one of my other clients. I just had the contract drawn up yesterday. His name is Roger Hart. He's new to the area and knows no one. He just fell in love with the town while driving through last year and decided to move here permanently. No wife, no kids—perfect, in other words."

"He sounds interesting, Lydia. Maybe it is time Tori made a new friend."

Lydia smiled conspiratorially and winked at Sharon.

"Shall we have them both to my house for dinner, say, Friday night?"

"Yes, let's!"

Sharon grabbed a notebook and started the menu for dinner at Lydia's house. Even though she just knew Tori wouldn't like their arranging this date, it was high time someone stepped in to help her. The two women had their heads close together as, deep into the night, they mapped out the details.

* * *

The first thing Tori noticed when she opened her eyes was that it was incredibly dark in the room, and then the pounding headache that was still in residence. Moaning, she eased herself from under the blankets and fumbled for the light switch. As she walked through the house, turning on a light in each room, she remembered the reason for sedating herself into a medicinal hangover. Though still saddened at Jim's forthcoming marriage and parenthood, she no longer felt like crying.

She put together a pot of coffee and ambled into the computer room vowing to try to get some work done. The first thing she noticed was that the screen-saver wasn't the same one she had chosen. This one was words, red Old English lettering raced across a white background. The backs of her arms broke out in goose bumps. Not taking time to try to read the complex calligraphy, Tori tapped the space bar, revealing what hid beneath there. Her eyes widened as she saw text there on the monitor, as if awaiting her approval.

Angry rain had assaulted the villa the entire day. Near dusk, the torrential downpour had abated into a magnificent rainbow. Mankala was walking with care around deep puddles, his master allowing the steed to go where he wished. Avery was too absorbed in his own thoughts, his own heart's desires, to be concerned which direction they traveled. He was lost in memory of the one who consumed his passion, his dreams. As he saw her in his mind, his breath caught at his chest in wonder. It was as if he could taste her lips, feel her body leaning into his, smell her essence, hear her voice whispered through the trees. Seabirds swooped and cried out, their mournful song matched that of his heart.

As Avery and Mankala ascended the crest of the largest hill on the property, he followed the arc of the multicolored hues as far as he eyes could see. It was here, near the end, that awaited his own share of gold, as promised in legends. There sat his lady, his love, atop an outcropping of craggy rocks, staring into the deepening twilight. At the sound of horse hooves, she expectantly turned to look for him. As she stood, waiting, his eyes filled at the sight of her beauty.

The seamstress had chosen well the color of the dress, green as a dew-kissed meadow. Stitched all around with small tucks and pleats to accentuate her breasts, it hugged her slender shoulders, clung to her waist, then fell to her feet in gentle swaths. The collar rose to meet the petal pink softness of her face, the color setting off her auburn hair like lace against copper. She was as fresh and sweet as the dawn.

As his master dismounted, Mankala dropped his head as if in greeting her. Avery heard the horse's whinny at his own pleasure of her presence.

If he had traveled with the tempo of his heart, Avery would have been running toward this exquisite creature, but he fought to restrain himself, for fear of frightening her away, as he always seemed to do. He didn't understand. He felt that she loved him as deeply, that her passion surged through her as strongly as his own, yet she never failed to run from him. Avery slowed his step even more as he neared her.

She stood there, the rain-fresh breeze playing with the folds of her dress, at times wrapping it more closely to her lovely form. It was as if Mother Nature herself were teasingly tempting him. She nervously flicked her tongue, wetting her lips, eliciting a moan he held beneath his breath. Her emerald eyes were large in her lovely face that was colored so sweetly with the height of a sweet blush. Her rapid, shallow breath caused her bosom to rise and fall most deliciously and Avery fought to keep his hands from her.

He smiled as he stood mere inches from her. Her head tilted back as she looked into his face, staring at his mouth, desire narrowing the pupils of her eyes. Avery felt the heat radiating from her, and his desire rose to meet it. Without a word, he leaned down, his lips cautiously touching hers. When she didn't pull away, he increased the pressure of his mouth, and was dizzily thrilled when he felt her lips part beneath his own. Tentatively, he touched her soft lips with his probing tongue, and felt the electrical reaction course through her body. Immediately, she jerked her head away, and turned to run down the hill.

Avery's shoulders sagged and his eyes filled with sorrow as he watched her run. Knowing it was of no avail, he held out his hand, begging her to come back to him.

"Come back, my darling! I love you! Please come back to me, Victoria."

Tori heard her own harsh breathing echo back to her from the walls of her computer room. She touched her forehead then quickly dropped her hand when she felt the cold sheen of sweat covering her face. Her arms crossed over her stomach as she felt a spasm seize through her middle. Instinctively doubling over, she fell into the familiar chair to read again the words she had *not* written. Over and over she retraced the text, always feeling apprehension as she neared the end, as if she were reading it again for the first time. No matter how many times she read it, her body wouldn't relax, refused to release her from this icy cold grip of foreboding. Folding her trembling hands in her lap, Tori struggled to make sense of this phenomenon. Thoughts raced through her mind, each one screaming to be heard above the others, colliding into each other, only to skitter away angrily when she refused to acknowledge it.

"What is this? What's going on here? I know I didn't write this. It's not even my style. O God, have I lost my mind? What the hell is the matter with me?"

Tears of frustration froze on her cheeks as she heard the deep sigh of sadness behind her. Her whole body felt alive with crawling insects as she swiveled around in her chair. As before, she saw no one, nothing, but she did feel heat emanating from a spot just behind her.

She grabbed her purse, then ran at breakneck speed to her car. She had time to think just before she screeched from the house. *I thought ghosts felt* cold.

* * *

Sharon pulled open the door, her sleep-disheveled hair around her head. She was completely awake, fear at being awakened at 3 A.M. wiping cobwebs of sleep from her mind. Her mouth was slack in surprise as seeing her daughter's blanched face and entire body shivering in terror.

"Honey! What is it?"

She pulled Tori into the house, closing the door and wrapping an arm around her daughter with the same movement.

"Baby, what's wrong?" Moving away only far enough to quickly check for blood or visible injuries, Sharon's own face was devoid of color. "Please Victoria, tell me what's wrong."

Embarrassed shame colored Tori's cheeks. Now that she was away from the phantasmal presence, she was already convincing herself she had imagined the entire incident. Of course, she couldn't erase the unearthly words on the computer monitor, but if she concentrated hard enough, she might be able to come up with some type of logical explanation.

"Mom, I'm okay, really I am. I just had a bad dream, and if you don't mind, I'd like to sleep over here the rest of the night. You know, wanting your mommy when you get spooked." Tori could tell that her laugh did nothing to relieve Sharon's feeling that something was wrong, very wrong. She knew a mother's instinct was a viable, real thing. She was thankful when her mother didn't press the issue.

"Well, of course you can stay here, Honey. You know you're always welcome to spend the night. I like having my little girl with me."

Tori grinned at the term "little girl" and her mother's look warned her to not push it. She hugged Sharon, said she was tired, and asked if they could just go to bed now.

* * *

Standing still in the vacated room, the glow of the computer cast no shadow on the wall as it shined against Avery's form. Nevertheless, the pain etched upon his face was real.

Chapter Eight

Tori was greeted with a cascade of brilliant sunshine lying softly on her face. Though she stretched languidly, her thoughts were already in high gear. It took a few seconds for her to find her bearings.

Where am I? This isn't my room. Oh yeah, I'm at Mom's. I came here last night after having the life nearly scared out of me. The book—ah yes, the book and words on the computer that I didn't even write. And then there was that... that thing standing behind me in the room.

An involuntary shudder traveled her spine and she threw off the blankets. She smelled the delicious aroma of coffee and breakfast before her feet hit the floor. At once, she was famished. Her mother had thoughtfully left a robe at the foot of the bed. Tori slipped it on, grateful for the warmth.

Sharon met her with a smile and a kiss.

"Good morning, Baby. How'd you sleep? I peeked in a couple of times and you seemed to be resting well."

"Oh, I slept like the dead. Hmm, bad terminology there. I mean, I slept like a log." Tori grinned at Sharon's look of amusement.

The two women talked companionably over waffles. They talked about anything except what had brought Tori to Sharon's at three in the morning.

"Tori, we need to talk."

"Mom, please. I don't really want to discuss it right now. I just want to get my head screwed on straight and go back home. I..."

Sharon covered Tori's hand with her own.

"No, Sweetheart, not about *that*. Lydia and I have done something I'm sure you're going to be mad about."

Tori paused in mid-bite, fork suspended in the air in front of her face, and looked at her mother warily.

"O God, what have you two done this time?"

Sharon held her stomach from laughing so hard.

"You should see your face. Oh, this is priceless. Wish I'd had a camera to get a shot of that!"

A lopsided grin met Sharon's laughter.

"Well, it's just that you scare me when you start a sentence like that. Are you two planning to overthrow the government? Start a nuclear war? Create rioting in the streets? I never know what happens when you and Lydia get together; it's always a shock to me."

"Oh, good grief. It's nothing that drastic, Honey. I know you hate it when we meddle in your life, but we thought you should get out of that house more. We thought it might even be a good idea if you..."

"If I... What? Come on, surely you two came up with a plan about how to 'fix' me."

Sharon hesitated in answering which made Tori nervous.

"Mom? What is it? You're worrying me now. Just open your mouth and spill the beans."

Sharon took a deep breath and plunged into the theory she and Lydia had devised. "We just feel it would be a good idea if you started seeing someone... a man. You need to get out of that gloomy house and enjoy life. Tori, there's more to life than books, even if you don't know that yet. If you dated, you could enjoy life instead of letting it pass you by. I know..."

Tori held up her hand.

"And do you two have a certain man in mind for this little experiment, someone devastatingly handsome to sweep me off my feet?"

"Well..."

Tori shocked her mother into silence by laughing out loud.

"Oh, this is hilarious! Not only have you figured out how to mend my lonely heart, you've actually found a candidate. Tell me, Mom, who is this lucky man?"

"Well, his name is Roger. Roger Hart. He's a writer, too. Lydia knows him because he just became one of her clients."

"Oh? What does he write?"

"He, uh, well, he writes science fiction."

"He does? How interesting."

Tori knew that her mother expected outrage and hurled remarks about them trying to control her life. She didn't fail to see the look of surprised relief on her mother's face.

"Really? You think that's interesting? I thought you believed sci-fi was a waste of the written word."

"I've grown up a little since I said that, Mom. I now admire all written works and the people who achieve their goals—live their dreams. But as far as you and Lydia setting me up for a blind date..."

"Oh, no! It wouldn't be like that, Tori. We're going to have a nice dinner and invite both of you over..."

"Wow, you've really got this all mapped out, don't you? Tell me, were you going to consult with me before you picked out the dinnerware pattern?"

Tori laughed again at her mother's look of indignant hurt.

"I'm only teasing you, Mom. Sure, this sounds like a good idea to me. What the heck? I might even like the guy."

"Really? You will? I never thought... Oh honey, I'm so glad you're doing this. It'll be good for you to meet someone. You might even fall in love and..."

"Whoa there, Nelly! You're putting the cart before the horse. How about just letting me meet the guy before you and Lydia arrange my wedding?"

Sharon stood to wrap Tori in her arms. She kissed the top of her head, then strolled across the room to call Lydia and finish the dinner plans.

Tori smiled around the next bite of food, listening to her mother's end of the conversation with the agent, she could tell that she had happily surprised both women by agreeing to this dinner date without a fight.

This isn't going to kill me. Heck, I might even actually have fun. Starting to date may be what I need right now. It just might help me get my mind off Jim and Shawna, and chase away whatever ghost is floating around my imagination. Hey, it couldn't hoit!

Tori continued munching as she listened to her mother smilingly tell Lydia that all systems were go.

* * *

The house didn't seem so frightening in the daylight. Tori squared her shoulders and walked into the computer room. Resolutely, she sat before the keyboard to see what new words had transpired since she had run from the house in terror. Somewhat amazed, she saw that no further words had been written in her absence. Sitting there, she began to question her own sanity.

Okay, nothing new here. It only happens when I'm in the house, supposedly asleep. Does this mean that it's really me that's doing all this? Have I lost it so much that I'm writing in my sleep and don't remember any of it when I wake up? If this is true... Oh, girl, you do need to get a life!

As was her habit lately, Tori began to speak out loud.

"I guess it's a good thing I'm going to meet this Roger person. If I'm lucky, he may just save me from myself."

Her chuckle was cut off by the sound of a crash in the living room. Tori ran to the source and saw that one of her lamps had overturned and was lying in the floor. She saw that she had left the door open and concluded a gust of wind had knocked the lamp off its base. She closed the door and almost mindlessly placed the lamp back to its original position before she headed back to the computer and her work.

If Tori hadn't been so preoccupied, she might have seen the semi-solid form standing there in the corner, glaring at her.

* * *

Tori stepped from the mounds of bubbles, then reached in to pull the plug. She stood watching the small whirlpool as the water emptied from the tub. Her mind was its own little dervish, planning her clothing choices for the dinner in a couple of hours. She was somewhat surprised to find she was actually looking forward to the evening.

The wire hangers scraped across the metal rod as she tried to decide what to wear. This was one of those rare occasions when she wished she had more dresses, although she knew that it would be obvious to her mother and Sharon that she was trying to impress Roger. Her only defense in life had always been an assumed nonchalance; she couldn't let her guard down now.

Pulling a pair of black slacks from the closet, she assembled them with a white sweater she had bought just a few weeks before.

Throw in a pair of black flats and ya got an ensemble. This is ridiculous. I don't really care what one Roger Hart thinks of me. Do I?

Tori applied a fine mist of body cologne before pulling her clothing over her still-damp body. Draping a towel around her shoulders, she walked to the bathroom to apply her make-up and try to tame the wild mass of red curls around her face. Holding a black clip against her hair, she decided it was just too "frou-frou" and threw it back in the drawer.

Little over an hour later, Tori declared to herself it was as good as it was gonna get, slung her shoulder bag over her arm, and practically glided out the door. After she turned the key in the lock, she threw the key ring up in the air and caught it with a smile on her face. She grinned all the way to the car.

* * *

He stood there, jealousy and anger running rampant through his heart. The very idea that *his* Victoria was meeting a man drove him into a near frenzy. She loved him... *him*, damn it! But with this form in which he was trapped, he couldn't show her just how much she loved him... needed him. He could feel changes taking place, that he was becoming... something. He somehow felt that, when she needed him the most, he would become a solid being for Victoria. Gritting his teeth, Avery only hoped it wouldn't be too late.

Chapter Nine

The warm light pouring through the windows of Sharon's home was beckoning. With a knot in the pit of her stomach, Tori walked slowly toward the door. Now that the actual moment to meet Roger had arrived, she was a bundle of nerves. What if he was ugly? What if he was insipid? What if he was handsome? What if he was handsome, exciting, and didn't like her? Not giving herself more time to ponder this and become even more nervous, Tori smoothed her hair, took a deep breath, and opened the door with a smile on her lips.

"Hello, everyone. Something smells delicious!"

The only male in the room had been sitting on the sofa, but rose when Tori walked into the room. Wearing a dazzling smile, he extended his hand.

"And you must be Victoria. I'm sorry; I was told you want to be called Tori. Tori. It's a pleasure to meet you. My name is Roger Hart."

"Roger, how nice to meet you at last. I've heard many good things about you and your writing."

Tori glanced at her mother and agent. With an imperceptible shake of her head, she warned them to not voice the fact that she actually knew very little about the man because she hadn't seemed that interested in finding out. Both women wore a conspiratorial grin.

Lydia was the first one to insinuate a touch of reality.

"Forgive me for seeming to rush into this, but dinner is ready. I don't want to have the cheese soufflé fall while we stand here chit-chatting."

Roger pulled Tori's chair out for her and the two older women stood to the side, beaming. As he turned to help Sharon and Lydia into their chairs, Tori smiled at them both.

In spite of herself, she grinned at the two most important people in her life. No matter how hard she tried, she could never be angry with them. After all, their intention was to see that Tori was happy. Who could be upset with that logic?

As the meal progressed, it gave Tori time to study Roger, as she was sure he was doing the same. She had to hand it to him; he was charming, witty, and intelligent. Relegating them with anecdotes about his writing career had them all laughing. Not even his horror stories concerning former agents ruffled Lydia's feathers, which Tori would normally find impossible to fathom. It could have been that she remembered this man was a client, or perhaps it was Roger's extraordinary good looks that held Lydia's temper at bay.

And, oh, but was he handsome! The only feature Roger had that Tori dismissed was his blonde hair. She had always leaned toward dark men. His eyes were a disturbing color of metal-gray, the same shade as the storm-ravaged sky. He was tall. Tori estimated him to be around six-foot-three. His tan, even in the midst of winter, spoke of someone who spent a great deal of time outdoors. That would also explain his rugged physique. His shoulders were wide and his torso tapered into narrow hips that proudly displayed a firm backside. Tori blushed at her own thoughts.

It was as if Lydia read her mind, for as she stood to get the dessert, she leaned near enough to whisper in Tori's ear, "A lean, mean sex machine." Tori could feel the heat rush into her face, setting it on fire. Roger chose to act as if he hadn't noticed.

"So, Tori, tell me about your work. What do you like to write? How many books have you had published? I'm certain you've already heard I write science-fiction, but don't hold that against me." His laughter was deep and rich in texture.

They became so engrossed in discussing their writing, neither one noticed when the two older women left the room. It took Lydia clearing her throat in the other room to bring them back to reality. The conversation stopped in mid-sentence, they grinned at each other, then joined Sharon and their agent in the living room.

Soon afterward, Lydia's antique grandfather clock chimed, announcing for all who were interested, that is was eleven o'clock. The look of surprise on Roger's face was genuine.

"I had no idea it was that late. Ladies, please forgive me. I became so enchanted with all of you that I may have worn out my welcome."

Lydia waved his protests away with the sweep of an elegant hand.

"Oh Roger, chill out. It's not all that late. If you had worn out your welcome, I would've been the first one to tell you. Just ask Tori and Sharon." Her husky laugh made Roger grin.

"Well, I need to be going, anyway. I had hoped to knock out the outline for my next book before midnight. I somehow doubt I'll reach that goal now. Lydia, thank you for a wonderful dinner. I look forward to working with you this week. Sharon, a joy to have met you. He turned to Tori and took her hand between his own, "I hope that we may get together again. Maybe go to a movie after dinner some night soon."

Feeling her two matchmaker's eyes on her, Tori smiled and said she would like that, she would like that very much, and gave Roger her home telephone number. She walked him to the door, waved at him as he walked to his car, then turned to both ladies, a mischievous grin on her face.

"So, are both of you happy, now? You got what you wanted. I'm going to see him again."

Sharon said, with her face blushing, "Oh, it didn't really matter all that much to me, Dear. You know, if you liked him, and if you wanted to see him..."

Lydia held no such qualms about being bluntly honest.

"Yes, I'm happy, and so is your mother. It's high time you started dating. God, you'll be an old maid if you don't do something soon. And it just might improve your disposition, young lady."

If possible, Sharon blushed more profusely. "Tori, darling, I didn't..."

Tori held up her hand. "Mom, it's okay. Lydia is right in saying I need to meet someone, go out on dates. I don't think, though, that I can qualify for 'old maid' status since I have been married. I want to thank you both, honestly. This may be the beginning of a nice friendship. As for more... we'll have to wait and see, won't we?"

Sharon and Lydia both hugged their young charge, and Tori hugged them back fiercely.

"Since it's so late, and I seem to be so old in Lydia's eyes, I think I'll go home and go to bed. It's been a long, eventful day for all of us. I love both of you. And I'm so grateful to have you meddling in my life."

At their look of shocked innocence, Tori giggled as she walked out the door.

* * *

The morning after the dinner party, cold rain drenched the countryside, promising to mature into snow before the day ended. Tori shivered and pulled the blanket under her chin. It seemed like her whole body was shaking. She wondered if she had a virus, if she may have infected Lydia and Sharon, and how could she have gotten so ill so quickly.

How she dreaded getting up, but she had too. Tori needed to kick up the thermostat, grab a couple of aspirin, then run back to the warmth of her bed. She would forego the pleasure of a hot cup of coffee for now, knowing she wouldn't want to stand on the cold linoleum as she measured out the scoops of coffee. She made a mental note in her feverish brain, at the first opportunity, to buy one of those coffee pots with an automatic timer. Taking a deep breath, Tori dissolved into a fit of coughing. With knees drawn up, she turned her face into the pillow, and harsh, hacking sounds filled her aching ears. When the spasms passed, she took short, shallow breaths.

"Lord, I won't do that again."

The minute she removed the blanket, her entire body shivered from head to toe. Bracing against the draft of simply walking through the house, she rose tremulously to her feet. Leaning against the cool surface of the wall, she fought to clear her fuzzy vision so she could be sure the furnace was still working. Her teeth clinched tightly against the chill rippling her skin. Tori expected to see icicles clinging to the thermometer dial, yet saw that it was seventy degrees. Giving the dial a twirl, she stumbled to the bathroom in search of aspirin.

Her hands were shaking so badly that she dropped half the pills on the counter. Tori scooped up four and washed them down with water from the tap. She closed her eyes against the steady drip that she still hadn't had repaired. Each drop that hit the porcelain hammered through her aching head. She leaned against the mirror behind the sink. The cold glass was soothing on her hot face. She didn't know how long she stood there; time seemed to have lost all meaning. Tori shuffled back to bed, falling among the blankets, pulled them to her forehead, and finally fell into a feverish sleep.

At some point, Sharon called. Tori must have been lucid enough to carry on a brief conversation, for her mother didn't sound alarmed. Nothing was mentioned about illness, headaches, or fever. If her mother had known, Tori knew she would come over immediately. As much as she loved her, Tori didn't want her mother hovering over her now. All she wanted was to shut out the world and sleep.

The fever raged on. Unknown to Tori, at times it was dangerously high. She thought someone was placing cool washcloths on her hot head. Each time, she smiled in gratitude. She even imagined she felt a hand stroking her face. When she reached up to caress the comforting hand, her fingers touched coarse hair, and she murmured Jim's name.

For three days Tori lapsed in and out of consciousness. She was delirious with fever and mumbled words of appreciation whenever her head was lifted from the sweaty pillow so that she could sip from the glass of delicious water to wash down the pills that had been put into her mouth. She would squint her hot eyes, trying to focus on Jim's face as he leaned over her. But the room was dark and the hallway light shining against his back created a silhouette, so she couldn't see very well. She forced a smile, touched his face, and fell asleep again.

As the fever raged on, she thought she was dreaming when she felt a hand holding hers. She awakened enough to feel something cool being slipped onto her finger. Her hand seemed so heavy as she lifted it to see the way lamplight gleamed from the gold band. She didn't know how it got there, but she knew there was an inscription inside. As she fell back into a stupor, she imagined she heard a voice whisper in her ear.

"I pray she was right when she promised the ring holds magic. If so, you will not only recover quickly but one day you will love me as I love you: with all my heart, forever."

Just as the sun was slipping over the horizon on the fourth day, Tori opened her eyes, wincing against the sore muscles of her back. In the semi-gloom of her bedroom, she felt a presence near her. She turned her head, and there, beside her was a man. He was lying on his side; his arm was bent to rest his head on his hand as he looked into her eyes. The image was vague, billowy, yet she made out his form. It then occurred to her that she could see *through* him, to the window next to the bed. Instantly, her heart started fluttering in her chest and she began to tremble. This couldn't be true; it wasn't possible.

"Avery?"

A hesitant but loving smile, "Victoria, my love..."

Tori fainted.

Chapter Ten

Tori awoke with someone gently slapping her face. Her body tensed rigidly before she got her bearings.

"Mom? What are you doing here?"

At once, bits of information came flooding into her memory. She was so intent trying to remember she missed some of her mother's words.

"...so I came over here to see if you're all right."

"I'm sorry, Mom, what did you say?"

Sharon sighed. "I said that I had the strangest feeling something was wrong with you, so I came over here to see if you're alright. Tori, how long have you been sick?"

Absentmindedly, Tori replied while she glanced around the room.

"Oh, for a couple of days now. It wasn't that bad, Mom, honest. I had a headache and may have been running a slight fever. Nothing to get all upset about. I'm better now; I think I may just live after all." She forced herself to look at her mother and offered as good a smile as she could muster.

"Gee, wonder why I don't believe you, Dear?" Sharon took Tori's hand to stare at the ring on her left hand. "This is beautiful, Tori. Where did you find such an exquisite ring?"

"It's just costume jewelry, Mom. I ran across it when I was looking in a small shop in town. I thought it was pretty and the price was right, very cheap, so I bought it."

Tori threw back the blankets, *when did she put the extra ones on the bed?* and stood up to prove she was feeling okay. Her head began to swim and she fell back across the rumpled bed. She closed her eyes and covered them with her hand, fighting down the nausea that threatened to overcome her.

"Ah, yes, I can see that you're just fine, Tori. Why didn't you call me?"

"Mom, in case you haven't noticed lately, I am now an adult. I did just fine. I took care of myself."

"How long has it been since you've eaten?"

"Oh, a few hours, I guess."

Sharon tugged Tori's body around so that she was lying back on her pillow. She pulled the first two blankets over her daughter.

"Yeah, right. I'm going to fix you some tea and make some toast. You'll have to start out small, but you'll be eating real food soon. Just rest. Do not, repeat, do not, get out of this bed. I'll be back in a few minutes."

Tori raised her head from the pillow. "I really should get up and work on the book. I haven't done anything for the last few days. I'm going to get behind schedule."

Sharon looked at her worriedly. "Tori, I went first to your office, looking for you there. Honey, you *have* been working. There's quite a bit of new material there, or so it seems to me."

Tori moaned and fell back against the bed.

O God, it's happened again. What's wrong with me?

"Honey, are you okay?"

"Yeah, Mom, I'm fine. How about that tea now? That sure sounds like a good idea to me."

She closed her eyes to signify she was tired, and Sharon bustled from the room. From the kitchen, Tori heard the sound of pots and pans clattering to the floor and her mother's whispered oath. She grinned, then her mouth fell as she remembered that new material had been written while she was sick. It was possible she had forgotten, but she didn't remember writing one word for almost a week now. So, if not her... who did? And what was that thing she had seen... or what she *thought* she had seen? All of this just wasn't within the realm of reality. To consider the possibilities made her head feel worse, dizzier.

* * *

Sharon spent the next two days with her daughter. Only then did she feel comfortable leaving Tori alone. She supervised as Tori ate a bowl of hot soup and drank all her milk before she would go home.

"Now, you promise me, if you need anything, anything at all, you'll call me right away? Promise, or I'm not leaving."

Tori stood to kiss her mother's cheek. Holding up her left hand, she placed her right one on her heart.

"I, Victoria Lynn Stanfield, do solemnly promise to call my mommy if I need anything, anything at all."

Sharon's grinned, then chuckled.

Tori walked her mother to the door, hugged her as she expressed her gratitude, then leaned against it with a sigh as she heard Sharon's car engine start. She had forced herself to not look at her computer while her mother was in the house. She now felt as if she would explode if she didn't read what was written there.

She took a deep breath and threw her shoulders back, yet her fingers trembled as she cleared the screen saver. Her eyes grew large and her face ashen as she gripped the edge of the desk, reading the words waiting for her.

As he sadly watched Victoria run away, Avery's eyes again filled with tears. He didn't understand how he could love someone who brought him such heartache. He leaned his head onto the dampness of Mankala's mane, and the horse, too, dropped his head in sympathy.

Avery lifted his head skyward, asking, pleading, that she be sent back to him. He implored that he couldn't live without her, that he loved her beyond all others. Was there no way to make her realize this?

Avery jerked his head around as he heard a rustle of leaves, the stealthy snapping of twigs beneath a foot. Alert against intruders, he pulled his gun. Mankala's head lifted and he snorted with anxiety, sensing his master's tenseness. Avery laid a quiet hand on the horse's flank for silence. With gun readied, Avery watched as the tree branches parted and she stepped forward.

With a sigh of happiness, he dropped the gun and jumped from the horse.

"My darling, my Victoria."

Once more looking heavenward, he whispered, "Thank you."
As he gazed upon her, Avery knew he had never seen anyone
as beautiful as she. Her dash through the woods had caused her
hair to fall free and it tumbled about her shoulders, cascading to
the middle of her back. How he longed to plunge his hands into
the fieriness of those lovely curls. He could almost imagine the
texture of her hair winding around his fingers, as she had
wrapped herself around his heart.

He walked toward her, his heart beating faster with each slow
step that closed the distance between them. He no longer heard
the birds singing, or the wind dancing its way through the rustling
leaves, or Mankala's whinny of pleasure. All he could hear, all he
could see, all he could fathom was Victoria.

Avery didn't understand why their times together were so
brief, why she seemed so frightened of him, or why each time he
touched her she ran from him. He didn't understand why he felt
as if he didn't even exist until she was with him. At this moment,
he wasn't going to waste time pondering any of that; he just
wanted to cherish the sight, the smell, the feel of her.

As she moved nearer to him, Tori didn't understand what was
happening or why she kept having this same dream. Yet it felt
more than a dream, more like an actual occurrence. She felt as if
she could reach out and touch him, feel the texture of his skin,
taste the smooth silk of his lips, hear his sigh if he were to lie
beside her. Not only did it feel real, it felt right.

She ached with longing, to touch him, kiss him, hold him
tightly against her, yet something undefined held her back. Her
body felt charged with a painful current, and her body thrummed
with electricity that only his contact could alleviate. The more she
yearned to lie with him, the farther she pulled away. Not even she
knew why she denied herself such passionate release, but
Victoria only knew it couldn't be allowed to progress any further;
she couldn't allow her emotions, her lust, free reign.

The ringing of the telephone broke Tori's concentration.
She vowed once again to remember to turn the ringer off the

next time she was writing. It's just that so few people called that she forgot, till one of the few never failed to call while she was busy. With a deep furrow between her eyebrows, she lifted the telephone receiver, her eyes never leaving the computer monitor, or the words she was still reading.

"Yes? Hello?" Her tone of voice was distracted, irritated.

Lydia's throaty laugh echoed back to her.

"And good day to you, Luv. Are we in a cranky mood?"

"I don't know how *you* are, but I may be a little on the cranky side, yes. You English... always using the 'we' in your conversation. This is a solitary emotion, dear."

"Oh my, you are in a mood. Well, I might as well hang up and not bother to tell you about a handsome man who wants to take you to dinner, right?"

Tori's eyes left the screen to stare at the mouthpiece of the phone as if she could see Lydia's grinning face staring back at her in amusement.

"Are you talking about Roger Hart?"

"The one and only. It would seem that the very eligible, and terribly handsome, Mr. Hart was quite taken by you at dinner the other night. We went over his contract this morning and he just, oh-so-casually mentioned that he may call to invite you to dinner. I, of course, encouraged him to do so. I told him that it'd been months since our sweet little Tori had made love..."

"O my God, you didn't!"

Lydia erupted into guffaws of laughter.

"I swear, Tori, you are so easy to get to. Of course I didn't, you goose. When he made his comment that sounded more like a question, I asked him if he had your telephone number. He said he did, and wondered if you'd be interested. My answer was you wouldn't have given him your number if you hadn't been."

"To be honest, I'm not sure why I did that. It was impulsive, and really unlike me. I rarely give my phone number to men I've just met. I guess I thought if you knew him, it would be okay."

"Yes, darling, it's okay. Now, be a good girl and answer the phone politely when he calls. Don't be reading your own words on the computer and appear disinterested when he calls, like you did just now with me. 'Bye, love. Talk to you soon."

Tori hung up the phone, staring at the wall, wondering so many things about one Mr. Roger Hart.

* * *

The next afternoon, Tori was diligently working on the book. She had her hair up in a long, curly ponytail that hung out the back of her baseball cap. A small MP3 player sat beside her computer and sounds of Motown ricocheted off the walls of her office. She'd been making notes on paper for ideas on the ending of the novel when the phone rang. She'd picked it up and mumbled a greeting before realizing she still had the pencil stuck between her teeth. Knowing the person on the other end of the line couldn't see her; Tori nevertheless blushed as she removed the damp pencil to lay it on the desk.

"Tori?" It was a resonant male voice that she didn't immediately recognize.

"Yes?"

"Hi! This is Roger Hart. We met at your mother's house for dinner a few nights ago?"

Unconsciously smoothing a stray lock of hair, she sat up straighter in her chair, pulling her eyes from the work in front of her.

"Of course, Roger, how are you?"

"I'm fine, thank you. I was calling to ask if you'd like to go to dinner sometime soon?"

"Dinner? Sure, that sounds great. When do you want to do this?"

He chuckled in her ear; the sound was pleasing.

"Well, I know this is bold, but I was hoping we could go tonight. That is, if you're not busy, and if you don't already have another date, another commitment. If you do, I'll understand. I am being pretty presumptuous here, I know, but..."

Tori couldn't help but stifle a giggle.

"Roger, it's alright. Yes, tonight would be fine. I have no other commitment, and I just happen to have an opening on my rather busy schedule. Where are we going?"

"Good. That's great. How about that new restaurant in Forrest Springs—Jerome's?"

"Yeah, that would be just fine. I've heard a lot of good stuff about that place and I've been meaning to try it. What time? About seven?"

"Sure, that works for me. Now, I need directions to your house. I'm afraid if I ask Lydia, she will still be talking tomorrow."

Tori laughed at the shared knowledge of their literary agent and gave him simple directions.

"Thanks Tori. I'll see you at seven."

Tori laced her fingers behind her head and leaned back. She was smiling into thin air until her chair flipped back and she landed unceremoniously on the floor in a tangle of red hair, flannel-plaid arms and denim-covered legs. Her Tennessee Volunteers baseball hat sat askew on her head. She was in such a good mood, she could only laugh.

She rose awkwardly, still grinning.

"Hmm, wonder what one wears on a first date with a devilishly handsome man to an upscale restaurant? Ah yes, my new green blouse with black pants. I can wear that ring I bought at the boutique to go with the blouse. Yes!"

She only then realized she wasn't excited, as much as nervous, about this date.

Steam rising like a dragon's hot, angry hiss, the bathtub bubbled with fragrant scents. Tori sat on the side of the tub, humming her favorite song.

"Hmmm, Hmmm, where are you, with a love, oh so true...?"

She didn't notice the darkening of a shadow in the corner behind her, or feel the heat of emotion that simmered there.

Chapter Eleven

Roger was nothing, if not punctual. Precisely at seven P.M. he was ringing Tori's doorbell. He watched as her slim shadow approached the door, saw her hesitate on the other side, seeming to square her shoulders before she opened it. He pulled on his most dazzling smile so it would be the first thing she noticed. He'd been told his boyish face was disarming and his motives deceptive when he smiled this way.

As she stood there, incapable of realizing the effect she had on his libido, she caused him to inhale sharply, quickly, silently. Roger knew from previous research that the pupils of his eyes were becoming dilated in direct response to a stirring beneath his pants zipper.

God, how he wanted to take her right there, right then, without ceremony, without excuses. But abiding by society's rules, he would wine and dine her, then approach this little matter later tonight.

"Tori, you look lovely, as always. Are you ready, or should I step in for a minute to wait?" He purposely forced a benign expression onto his face.

"No, that's alright, Roger. I'm ready to go if you are."

"Of course, Milady, as you wish."

Tori smiled at his use of the verbiage in her own writing and stepped through the open door. Just as Roger was pulling it closed behind them, there was a sound much like a hoarse moan, or a groan of building anger. He quickly turned his head, peering back into the house, his mouth a round "O". Tori placed her hand over his that still held the doorknob and gently pulled the door closed.

"Old houses, Roger, make some weird noises, don't they?"

He grinned as he walked her to the sleek, low-slung sports car waiting at the curb, his hand resting against the small of her back. It was a gesture that Roger knew some women found intrusive, yet sensual, at the same time. He relied on it to see which way the currents were running. If the woman pulled away, he knew to back off, give her more time and space. If she didn't, he smugly assumed all systems were go. Tori drew away from his touch and his radiant smile slipped just a notch. Thinking this was now a challenge, Roger smiled even wider, anxious to get the charade of dinner over so he could get her back home and begin to thaw her out. No woman resisted him for long, willingly or otherwise.

He had made reservations at the five-star, dimly lit restaurant that encouraged intimacy and had a great menu. Roger planned to eat light; he didn't want to seduce Tori on a full stomach. He grinned lasciviously as he walked behind her to their table. He wiped the expression from his face when she turned to smile at him before she sat down.

"Tori, I hate to repeat myself, but you are absolutely beautiful. How that husband of yours was stupid enough to let you go... Well, his loss is my gain. I'm sure every man in the room is jealous of me."

* * *

Even though she was smiling, Tori felt anything but comfortable. She had looked forward to this evening as it had been so long since she'd been on a date. She had anticipated lively, intelligent conversation with a handsome man, a fellow writer. But, before they had even reached his car, she was beginning to feel somewhat ill at ease. This man who had charmed her mother and agent made her feel apprehensive, and she had caught the look that made her feel as if she were standing before him naked. It wasn't anything she could actually put her finger on, but all at once, the idea of being out with Roger didn't seem like such a good idea.

Oh, he was still being the charming, attentive host. He pulled Tori's chair out for her, smiled at her as he seemingly hung onto her every syllable. He was making conversation, keeping it lively and humorous. Still, there was this nagging feeling in the back of her mind, something just wasn't right here. All she wanted to do now was get dinner over with as pleasantly, as quickly, as possible and then go home. Strangely, her stomach grew queasy when she thought of his walking her to her door.

When the waitress came to take their order, Roger made small, flirty remarks to her. Evidently, the young woman was used to this type of behavior, but it made Tori squirm in her seat with embarrassment.

"Good evening, folks. How are you? Are you ready to order? Our special tonight is the prime rib, served with baked potato and salad. Do you see anything you like on the menu?"

Roger looked up into her face. "No, there's no pretty little blonde waitress on the menu. I need to speak to the manager at once. It's unbelievable that he should leave the second most tempting dish off the menu. The first would be my beautiful date here."

Tori blushed as she stared at her menu, trying to avoid looking at Roger's face. She knew he thought he was funny, that his comments were cute. She thought him immature and disrespectful.

"My lovely companion here will have the prime rib, cooked medium-well, and the salad with the house dressing."

Tori knew her mouth was open and that her jaw was slack.

"That's okay with you, isn't it, Honey?"

Tori bristled at his too-familiar term of endearment. She could create a terrible scene, verbally, and try to embarrass him as he had just done to her, or she could acquiesce like an adult. Glancing at the young woman waiting to take their order, Tori felt as if they had already caused her enough trouble.

The smile felt as artificial as it was. "Yes, that will be fine. Thank you."

While Roger ordered his own food, smoked salmon with a side dish of rice, Tori was clenching her hands in her lap. She ached to reach over and slap his arrogant face. His condescending attitude and his assumption he was so attractive he could get by with such behavior, infuriated her. She found she liked him less with each passing minute. What were her mother and agent thinking? Surely they didn't realize he was such a conceited, overbearing boar. To be honest with herself, she had to admit the man she had dinner with at her mother's house and the man with her now were two different people. Lydia obviously knew little about her newest client. In spite of herself, Tori chuckled as she imagined how Lydia would tear into this pompous ass seated across from her, looking so smug with himself.

"What is it, Tori? C'mon, share with me. You're grinning like you have an inside joke." Roger was smiling, waiting for the punch line, and Tori so wanted to give it to him.

"Oh, it's really nothing. I was thinking about something my mother had told me about some friends of ours. It really wouldn't interest you. You'd have to know these people for it to be funny. So, tell me about your latest project, Roger. How is your book coming along?"

Roger groaned, "Are we honest to God going to talk 'shop' tonight? I thought we'd go out, have a nice dinner, and get to know each other better, perhaps grow closer."

Tori's eyebrows wrinkled. "Well, isn't this the way to get to know each other better? I mean, we're both writers, so that's a common ground to start with. But, if you don't want to talk about that, what do you want to talk about?"

"How about our first sexual experience?"

Tori again looked at her hands clinched into fists in her lap. "No, I don't think that's something I want to talk about. First of all, that's a very private subject—one I don't discuss with other people. Second of all, it's none of your business. You know, Roger, I think this date was a bad idea."

Roger reached his hand across the table so quickly he knocked over her glass of water.

"Oh, damn! I'm sorry. Damn it! Tori, I apologize. I didn't mean to make you uncomfortable." He dabbed at the spreading water stain on the linen cloth. "I just feel relaxed with you. Maybe I feel too relaxed. I'm sorry. I didn't mean to offend you. Please, let's change the subject and start over."

Their food arrived and conversation was stilted throughout the meal. Several times Roger attempted to draw her out, but he quickly reverted to using lewd, suggestive remarks.

When the last of the dishes had been taken away, Roger looked at her with a frown. "I don't know what else to do to make you happy. I've apologized and tried to keep the conversation flowing..."

Tori could feel the heat rising in her face. "Oh, please, Roger. Your conversation has consisted of nothing but dirty little comments meant to see how far you can go, to see if you're going to 'score' later. Let me put your mind at ease. It ain't gonna happen, Babe."

Roger' face reddened to an apoplectic shade of crimson. "Why, you ungrateful... Here I am, trying to be a nice guy by doing our agent a favor. She told me that you couldn't get a date, and asked me to take you out, show you some attention..."

Tori tried to remain calm and display some dignity as she rose from her seat. "Would you please take me home now? If you don't want to do that, I can call a cab."

"Oh, for God's sake, sit down, Tori. Stop being so damned melodramatic. There's no reason to get all bent out of shape over this. We started off on the wrong foot but there's no reason we can't salvage the night."

Quietly, firmly, "Now, Roger. I'm leaving—now."

Sighing heavily, Roger stood and threw some bills on the table. He took her arm as they left the table, but Tori jerked it out of his hand. She didn't wait for him to open her car door and hugged the handle as they drove away from the restaurant. She was only glad she didn't live so far away that they had to make more conversation. The temperature in the car was glacial, much colder than the sleet that fell on the windshield.

Tori was reaching for the door handle before Roger had come to a complete stop in front of her house. He reached out and took her hand and she froze, glaring at his gesture. She watched in the reflection of the dashboard lights as his face hardened.

"Oh no, Tori. I'm walking you to the door like a proper gentleman. I want Lydia to get the full effect when you tell her about our date. We're seeing this through to the bitter end, dear."

"There's no need for you to do that. I'm perfectly capable..."

Roger got out and stiffly walked around to open her door. Tori held her body rigid as he walked alongside of her, up the steps to her door. She could hear the dying leaves on the trees clacking dryly against each other. He stood silently as she fumbled with her key, then leaned lazily against the doorframe as the lock's tumblers fell into place.

Tori opened the door slightly, then turned to tell Roger goodnight and end the evening with as little additional anger as was now possible.

"Well Roger, I wish I could say it was fun, but..."

Roger pushed her against the open door, causing Tori to practically fall inside the house. As she was correcting her balance, she watched Roger close, then lock, the door behind his back. He had an evil grin marring his handsome face.

"Roger? What do you think you're doing?"

"I *know* what I'm doing, Tori. I'm coming in for a night cap."

"No, you're not. This whole night hasn't gone well and I just want it over with. Please, just leave."

His laughter was mocking, derisive, yet Tori noticed the tightening of his jaw, the nearly involuntary pinching at the corners of his mouth as his eyes darkened. "Do you realize just how much I spent on dinner?"

Tori's face blanched, then turned pink. She repeated his words in astonishment, "Do you realize just how much I spent on dinner? You have got to be kidding me. No one uses that line anymore; it's antiquated, Roger. Here, I'll give you the money for my dinner. Whatever you spent, what was it, twenty bucks or so?" She opened her purse, fishing for her wallet.

Roger's lip curled into a thin, obscene sneer as he slapped it from her hands in one savage movement. "I don't want your damned money, girlie. However, you *can* repay me. I'm open to the bartering system."

"I do not believe this! Roger, get out of here immediately. Don't make this worse by forcing me to call the police. And I will, Roger, I promise you that."

His mouth compressed into a thin line of barely repressed rage and a whisper of fear washed over Tori's body. He took a couple of deliberate steps toward her, already bringing his hands up to grab her. There was something sinister smoldering in his now-obsidian eyes, something that scared her.

"You women are all alike. You want it as bad as we do, but you want to play hard to get. But, you know what? I've found out it ain't so hard to get. You just gotta show her how much she wants it. So, the choice is yours, Tori. We do this hard, or we can take it nice and easy. How do you like it, Tori? I'll bet you like it hard." A cold smile played along his professionally whitened teeth.

Tori's body betrayed her by beginning to tremble and sweat dotted her forehead. The grin on Roger' face turned menacing. Tori took a step backward, instinctively. She bumped her hip against the arm of her recliner and fell to the floor. As she scrambled for a handhold on the carpet, Roger was already bending over her. Tori was more frightened than she'd ever been in her life. Roger's face darkened and the smile that curved his lips sent a shiver of terror across her spine.

"No, Roger; please don't do this. Please..." The words were a mewled whisper in the deathly quiet room.

Unheeding of her words, Roger had one knee on each side of her trembling body. His breathing was harsh, sour, and spittle from his open mouth fell onto her cheek as he leaned his face closer. Tori closed her eyes and pushed against his chest with all her strength.

Suddenly, it seemed as if the air grew heavy and it shivered around her. At once she felt the weight of his body leave hers. It was as if Roger was propelled away from her. Her eyes flew open as she heard the thud of his body hitting the wall next to the locked door. He seemed to hang there, suspended, against the wall before his body slowly sank to the floor.

Even as she struggled to her feet, from the corner of her eye she caught sight of a heavy, luminescent haze. A translucent image, more like an impression, of a man loomed over the prostrate Roger. She felt, rather than saw, the angry stance of her rescuer. Fiery loathing seemed to emanate from this vaporous shape, yet Tori felt no fear for her own safety. She somehow understood the anger was directed toward Roger, alone.

The look of stunned disbelief might have been comical under other circumstances. Roger's mouth was open, his eyes were darting around the room and his face was a pasty white. His lips were moving, working to speak, yet no words came out. Staring at Tori with widened eyes, he scrambled sideways, his hands making slapping noises against the wall as he fought his way to the front door, his head turned to watch the vaporous form move closer. He managed to get to his feet, only to have them appear to be pulled from beneath him. His bottom hit the floor with a resounding thud that shook the lamp on the table beside him. Roger threw out his hands as if to fend off an attacker, the fingers splayed in a gesture of supplication. He fixed his gaze on a point just in front of him, but dared to allow his pleading eyes to look at Tori for only a second.

Tori understood the facial expression, but not the reason for it. She kept looking at the empty space Roger stared into and could find no reason for his look of terror. His tongue, at last, found the ability to speak.

"Please... I didn't know, I swear. Just leave me alone and I'll go." He began to carefully move ever closer to the door as he continued to plead, "If I had known... She never said a word. She never told me..."

Tori's head was turned sideways, staring into the emptiness that Roger was addressing. She looked back at Roger as if to say, "You're nuts."

Roger's chagrined smile somehow frightened Tori more than his attack on her. His next words slammed through her and confusion gave way to terror.

"Thanks, Buddy. I promise you, I won't be back. If I'd known Tori..." He bolted for the door, jamming his shoulder against the frame in his haste to leave. He didn't bother to speak again to Tori.

As she heard the car engine roar into life outside, the heavy fog beside her began to dissipate. Tori was shaking her head in denial, her eyes round and large in her horror-stricken face.

Oh no, this isn't happening. It's not possible. Mama!

She grabbed her purse on her frantic dash to her car.

* * *

Sharon opened her door to a daughter who began babbling the moment she saw her mother's face. Tori threw her arms around her mother and began to cry.

"Baby! What's wrong? What's happened, Tori?"

Tori's sobbing words were incomprehensible. Sharon's tone of voice belied the fear she felt, the firmness of her words pushing back the hysteria.

"Victoria! Stop crying and tell me what happened."

Tori took a deep breath when she saw she was scaring her mother. She leaned over to pull a tissue from a box sitting on the coffee table. Understanding moved into Sharon's face.

"Tori? Did Roger force himself on you? Did he...?" She seemed incapable of finishing the question.

Tori smiled tremulously, "No, Mom, he didn't. Oh, he tried, believe me, he tried. And I think he would have actually raped me if..."

"If what, Honey? Tori, tell me what happened."

She knew her mother wouldn't understand.

Hell, I don't even understand. What just happened back there at my house?

"Let's just say that my self-defense classes paid for themselves tonight, Mom."

The worry lines in Sharon's face were now overlaid with anger. "That bastard! I'm calling the police. Who the hell does he think he is..."

Tori took the phone from Sharon's trembling fingers. Her own shaking hand made it difficult to not drop the phone. "No, Mom, just let it go. It's over, done. I don't think Roger Hart will ever try that again."

"But Tori, he shouldn't be allowed to get by with this. He should be arrested, put behind bars like the animal he is..."

Tori put her arms around Sharon, trying to calm herself as she quieted her mother. It was as it had always been between them. They comforted each other, their love generating a protective shield that enveloped them. The anger and tears yielded to wobbly smiles.

"Mom, mind having an overnight guest-again?"

Sharon kissed her daughter and pulled her into the kitchen to help make a pot of tea.

* * *

As Tori slept in the security of her mother's home, a dream wrapped her in its arms.

The horizon was draped with soft colors, the sun setting on a quiet land. He stood before her, silent, love and desire intermingling in his eyes. She smiled and it was all the invitation he needed.

He framed her face with his hands, permitting himself the luxury of sinking into her emerald eyes that sparkled with love.

"Victoria, how I've missed you. How I wish you would remain here, with me, so that I may always protect you. Here, in my world, I have the power to overcome men such as Roger Hart. I was nearly ineffectual in that physical battle in your world. If not for the superstitious fears of a bully, I would have lost. Here, I have substance, strength. Stay with me, Victoria. Remain, so I may love and shelter you."

Her tears glistened in the fading amber twilight. Taking his hand in hers, she kissed the fingertips. Sadness forced the tears to spill across her cheeks. She turned and walked away. His voice faded more with each step she took, melting into the time where it belonged. The last words she heard were filled with anguish.

"I love you, my Victoria, and I will wait..."

She awoke to voices raised in anger. She grinned when she recognized Lydia's strident English accent. She threw back the blankets and rushed out to see her agent, her best friend.

Lydia opened her arms to hug her. The warmth of her embrace surprised Tori. She knew that Lydia loved her like she was her own daughter, but she rarely displayed such deep emotion. She correctly assumed this was due to the fiasco of the night before.

"That ass is no longer a client of mine! I'm going to tear his contract into a million tiny pieces."

"Lydia, you know you can't do that."

"And why the hell can I not do that, Tori? I can do whatever..."

"No, dear friend, you can't, and you know it. It's not ethical or professional to cancel his contract with you because of me. It's a business, Lydia, and he could sue you for not fulfilling the contract."

Lydia stared at the wall as she considered what Tori had said. All at once, her face was wreathed in a mischievous smile.

"You're right, of course. I can't tear up the contract but I have other options. Such as, I'm sure that no one will be interested in Mr. Roger Hart's new book. Why, the response from publishers is going to be just crushing to poor, dear Roger. It may hurt him so badly it could possibly destroy his horribly inflated ego and he would be unable to write another word."

Tori stared at her agent in shock.

"No, Lydia. Surely you're joking. You can't do that to an author. I don't like the man but I think that would be so wrong. He may be a low-rent piece of crap when it comes to the way he treats a woman, but he is a talented writer. Please, if you care for me, don't do this on my behalf. I would be forever sorry that other people may be unable to enjoy his work."

Lydia sighed loudly and Sharon's face was covered with a proud smile.

"Even though I'm your mother, you still amaze me. You're a beautiful soul, Victoria. I'm honored to be your mother."

Tori's gaze traveled the room as her face emanated a pretty pink glow.

"Thanks, Mom."

Lydia leaned over to kiss the young woman on the forehead. She spoke in a gruff voice.

"I just gained even more respect for you, Luv." Then clearing her throat and raising her voice, Lydia asked for a drink. "If you don't have the makings for a decent martini and force me to drink coffee, at least pour a generous dollop of Irish crème in the cup."

Sharon and Tori chuckled and pulled Lydia into a familial embrace, both of them kissing her on her cheeks until the Brit joined them in the laughter.

The women all sat down at the table with a mug of coffee, sans Irish crème. Lydia grimaced with each sip she took. Tori got up and made a cup of tea. When she handed it to her, Lydia smiled her appreciation.

"Bless you, sweet Tori. Now, tell me how the new book is coming. Mr. Editor in New York is concerned about the deadline. You'll make it in time, won't you, dear?"

Tori hoped the other two didn't hear her gulp of air. She felt the sweat begin at her brow.

"Sure, I will! I've got another three months and the book's about 75% done. I don't see any problem with meeting the deadline. In fact, I'm leaving in a few minutes so I can get back to work."

"Marvelous. I'll stop worrying then. It's just that this is your shot at the truly big time and I don't want one single problem to stand in your way. Plus, it'd be a feather in my hat, too, if I have a client on the bestseller's list. You're going to be the one that does all that, Tori. This book is only the beginning, Dear."

"I'm going to work hard to live up to that, Lydia."

Sharon patted Tori's hand. "You'll do it, Honey. I just know you will."

Tori hugged them both before she left. With assurances that she was, indeed, going to have the book done before they knew it, she reminded each of them that she loved them. She was still smiling as she drove into her driveway.

Her mood was much lighter than when she had left the night before. She wasn't sure she understood what exactly had happened with Roger but she decided to just let it go. It wasn't possible that some sort of ectoplasmic man had come to her rescue, no matter what it looked like. To accept the notion would be one step closer to a padded room.

For all her protestations to the contrary, she approached her home with trepidation. It seemed to take an hour for the door to swing open as she stood at the threshold. The only thing she heard when she walked into the house was the heater, which was just fine with her.

She grabbed the remote and switched on the TV as she passed through the room. The volume was low because all she wanted was background noise that wouldn't disturb her train of thought.

The teakettle was whistling by the time she had slipped into her writing clothes. The loose knit pants and bulky sweatshirt felt as comfortable as an old friend. Even if she spilled a drop or two of her tea on her clothes, it wasn't a tragedy.

Tori hummed along with the faint strands of a commercial on TV as she danced into her office. When she saw the computer monitor her mouth fell open and tea sloshed out of the cup as she slammed it down on the desk. She fell into her chair, jarring her teeth together.

The Earl Grey grew cold and tears began to flow as she read the words that she hadn't written.

Katherine called Avery to her bed. He gently lowered himself to sit beside her faded body that had brimmed with vitality just six months earlier. His throat felt as if he had swallowed something too large and his lungs became constricted.

"Good morning, Mother. You're looking much better…"

Her benevolent smile stopped his words. It was time to face the truth because she was no longer going to allow anything less.

"Avery, my child, the light of my life and heart. Today will be a sad one for you and I'm sorry that I shall be the reason for that. No, please be silent and listen, yes, love?"

It was with great effort that she reached for his hand. He moved quickly to conserve her strength. As she held his large hand in her own delicate, pale grasp, she continued to smile.

"Do not weep for me, Son. I was blessed in this life. I was given a man that loved me above all others, a man that would have given his life to defend mine. I was blessed with a son that all mothers would have wished for, a son that grew to be a fine man, just like his father."

She reached into her pocket and brought forth a ring that she placed in his hand. When Avery began to protest she made shushing noises while maintaining her smile.

"There will be many women in your life, Avery, but there is only one that was created just for you. This ring belongs to her. There is magic in a ring created for the love of your life. Place this ring upon her hand and love her as your father loved me-for the rest of your life."

She pulled his arm down so she could kiss the fingers closed over the ring. "I love you, my darling boy." She let her eyes drift shut. Her smile remained even after she was gone.

Tori pulled a tissue from its box, then dabbed at her eyes. Her reaction to these words overrode the fear she had felt when she first came into the room. It was as if she felt the physical ache deep within her chest. Imagining the death of her own beloved mother caused her own heart to be squeezed in an emotional vise. She sighed deeply as she forced her attention back to the computer monitor.

He laid his head at her heart and was still for several minutes. When he felt her soul had time to float onward, he lifted his pale face to the heavens. The thick, plush velvet of the heavy draperies and the lush pile of carpet failed to absorb his wail of anguish. The pain and desolation were nearly too large for the mammoth room to hold. The sound was so pervasive, so large, even the sleeping pigeons were awakened and flew to various points of the village.

Though the piteous cries were loud, the release of emotions was short-lived. As quickly as the sobbing began it ended. He reigned in his outburst. In the aftermath, the silence was deafening.

Avery rose from the deathbed and turned to his mother's three maids crying softly as they stood in the shadows. He touched each of their folded hands.

"Would you please help me? I need to get her ready. Find her favorite gown." Under his breath but still audible, "This is going to be so difficult. Dear Mother, I miss you already."

He rubbed his hands across his cheeks to wipe away the evidence of his tears. He was happy that there weren't more people present to witness his weakness.

Tori's anguished cries were as loud in the solid world as they were in the fictional account of Katherine Norcross' death. In her own mind Tori envisioned making arrangements to bury Sharon. She imagined her mother's waxy countenance, her still, cold body dressed in the clothing that Tori had taken to the funeral home, and the brave front Tori would be expected to wear for everyone else. The perceived pain was almost more than she could bear. She wished she could reach out to Avery, to hold him in her arms, to offer him comfort and console his wounded heart.

"What am I thinking? Console Avery? Have I finally, truly, lost my mind? This is a work of fiction. Words that I didn't even write! O God, what's going on here? This isn't possible; it can't be real!"

She put her head on the edge of the desk, her tears turning to agonized sobs of fear and confusion.

"Am I so lonely or insane that I could write chapters of a book and not remember it? Do I have such a need to create my own perfect man that I've lost touch with reality? Please, God, tell me what to do. Tell me how to get back to normal, whatever that may be."

At this point her words became undecipherable. She lifted her head to stumble from the room. She buried her face in the pillows on her bed and once more cried herself to sleep.

* * *

He sat beside her on the mattress. He stroked her hair but he knew if she felt it at all through her wracking sobs, she would mistake the touch for merely a draft of wind.

If only I had more substance so that I could comfort you as you wish to comfort me.

I have learned so much while watching you, being near you. I can push the buttons on that strange machine to create words but I cannot make you feel my touch.

I would lie beside you and hold you in my arms until your tears dried and you smiled into my eyes. I would caress your slender shoulders and run my fingers through your fiery, soft curls. If only I was fully here, I would love your pain away.

Avery began to feel a heaviness in his body that was deeper than an emotional reaction to his feelings for Tori.

Chapter Twelve

At some point during the early morning hours, Tori left her bed and sat in front of her computer. She wasn't aware she'd done it. When she again awoke at her desk, her neck and shoulders screamed in protest.

"Okay, dammit, that's it! I've had it. I'm fed up with this crap! So, what to do about it? I need to talk to someone other than myself. I don't really think I'm crazy anymore. So Tori, who do you talk to about all this Twilight Zone junk? I wonder if there's an 800 number, maybe for a group called 'Ghostbusters R Us.' "

She walked to her bedroom, fell onto the side of her bed and pulled the phone book from the drawer in the nightstand.

He listened as Tori spoke to someone about her haunted house. He shook his head as she described cold spots, objects being moved, familiar voices calling her name when no one was there. He grinned at her humorous descriptive phrases. Avery was certain that whoever was on the other side of the speaking device must be laughing.

"Ah sweet, Victoria, if you only knew that the only haunting here is what you are doing to my heart."

The ghost busters arrived at the house early, long before Tori wanted to be awake, dressed, and genial to strangers. She knew all of them would be upset to be called anything other than parapsychologists. She'd just keep that term to herself. Tori offered them coffee and they carried it around with them as they worked.

They spent hours walking through the house, at times with their hands outstretched into thin air, their heads were nearly touching as they whispered to each other and casting sidelong glances into the shadowy corners of every room. They held instruments that emitted high-pitched squeaking noises when tested.

Phrases like *electromagnetic field, amorphous, astral plane,* and *discarnate entity* peppered their dialogue. Digital recorders were placed in different rooms for EVP or electronic voice phenomena. The technicians explained that many times words were captured on recorders when no one was present. It's the way a spirit tries to communicate with the living. Tori nodded as if she knew what the heck they were talking about.

"Where do you notice the most activity?"

"Activity?"

"You know—cold spots, hot spots, the feeling that someone is watching you, objects being moved, etc."

"Oh, in just about every room; however, the room I'm most concerned with is my office. That's the place that scares me the most. I'll go in there and find pages written for my new book that I didn't write."

James, the self-proclaimed director of the group, snapped his head around. Tori could imagine his ears perking up as he raised his eyebrows.

"Really? Perhaps it's automatic writing, with a modern technological slant to it. I've heard of it being done with pen and paper but I have to admit, I've never heard of it being done with a computer keyboard before."

"What is it, this automatic writing? Sounds weird to me."

"I would imagine it does sound strange but it's a more common occurrence than most people realize. Someone writes, or in your case perhaps, types without any conscious thought. We believe it to be a spirit writing through a living being."

Tori tried to smooth the frown that she could feel was furrowed between her eyebrows, but was unsuccessful.

"Uh, what?"

"A spirit has something to convey to you, a loved one, or just anyone who will listen. It could be that he or she left something undone, an injustice was done, or is trying to warn someone that disaster is coming."

"But this... man, for I'm certain it's male, is writing entire chapters of a historical romance. In essence, he's doing my job for me and scaring me more every time he does it."

"I don't have an answer for you there. Maybe he doesn't like your style or he's just trying to make sure you're accurate." He laughed too loud, too pleased with his own wit.

Tori stared at him until he understood the glare and stopped braying. Her footfalls were hard and her shoulders tight when she exited the room. She heard James sputtering an apology behind her.

Chapter Thirteen

"Hello?"

"Lydia, it's me, Tori. Did I wake you?"

"Yes, but it's okay. You know I'm usually still up at midnight but it's been a long day and I was tired. What's wrong?"

"Oh, nothing really."

"You're not like other women, Tori, calling me just to chat, especially at this hour. Don't tell me nothing's wrong. Don't you ever sleep anymore, Victoria?"

"I have a question, Lydia."

"And that would be...?"

"I'm thinking about taking up drinking full-time. Can you give me any advice? You know, share a few tips with the new kid chasing the booze wagon?"

"You know, love, if it weren't you saying these things, I..."

"I know, Lydia, I know. I'm sorry. I truly didn't mean to offend you or upset you. I'm an ungrateful wench."

"A wench, eh? Very old-worldly of you, Sweetheart. Okay, spill it. What's wrong? I'm awake now so you might as well open up. It's obvious you want to talk to someone."

"I'm scared, Lydia."

Tori could hear the bed sheets rustle and imagined Lydia sitting ramrod straight against the headboard.

"Scared? What's going on, Tori? What's happening? Is someone threatening you? Is that bastard Roger bothering you again? I'll hurt him so..."

Her subdued voice silenced Lydia faster than a shout of obscenities.

"No, Lydia. It has nothing to do with that slime-ball."

"Well then, what is it? C'mon Tori, don't make me drag this out of you. You're starting to make me nervous. You know I don't like to be nervous. It's why I drink."

"Uh-huh."

Lydia let that one slide.

"My house is haunted—or something."

"What? For the love of Pete, Tori!"

"No, really! There's something very spooky going on here."

"Define *spooky*, Tori."

She told Lydia everything then. She began with the instances of objects being moved, even thrown, the radio taking on its own personality, the times an unseen someone stood behind her, and even the cold and hot spots in various rooms.

As Tori expected, Lydia began to logically account for each symptom of the supposed haunting.

"It's an old house, Dear. The structure settles, getting all comfy on its perch. That would sometimes cause things to slide off a table or slip from a countertop. Of course you're going to have drafts of cold air. I'd be *surprised* if you didn't have many of them. And your stereo is nearly as old as the house. I'll buy you a new one. And all of us have felt as if someone were watching us, standing behind us, even following us from room to room. Frightening, unsettling, but not a ghost. Maybe you need to get some of those odd people to come in there to check it out for you. Just to put your mind at rest."

"I did, Lydia."

"Wow! Okay, so what did they have to say?"

"They said that I was nuts to hang around with you."

"Victoria..."

"Okay, okay. They hooked up all these wacky gadgets, had wires strung all over the floor and instruments held in their sweaty palms."

"Well, you sound positive about this experience. I'll assume they didn't find anything."

Tori gritted her teeth.

" 'Nothing conclusive' is how they put it, which means they found nuttin'. They did, however, have a couple of suggestions. Other than being committed to the loony bin, it was said I should find someone to 'channel', which is a fancy word for a psychic. Then I heard the term *cryptomnesia* used in conjunction to me and I got the definition out of James before I threw them out of the house."

"I'll bite. What does *cryptomnesia* mean?"

"It's knowledge that may be revealed without the person remembering its source. Sometimes the phrase is used to explain forgotten memories which only appear to be paranormal experiences."

"Well, alrighty then! I have no idea what the hell you just said, but okay."

Tori cleared her throat, took a deep breath, and then finished the story.

"Lydia, there was one thing I've left out of this—the strangest occurrence of all. My current book is nearly completed."

"But, darling, that's wonderful! Why do you sound so upset about this fact? This is great news!"

"I'm not the one writing the book, Lydia."

Tori had never known her agent to be speechless. She could hear the seconds ticking off her bedside clock as she waited.

"We're taking you to a doctor, a good doctor, not some quack. We'll get to the bottom of this, I promise you that! Now don't you worry, Tori, it's going to be okay, because I'm going to make it okay."

"No, Lydia, no doctor. I know that no one believes me; I've come to accept that. I just wanted to tell you about this so that you'll know why I've been acting more squirrelly than usual, and to help me hide it from Mom."

"Now, Tori, don't put me in this position. Sharon will know that something is wrong. She is your mother and you can't hide from a mother's intuition."

"With your help, I can. If you love me, help me. If this book takes off as you think it will, I'll have enough money to move out of this old house. Then everything will be okie dokie once again."

"But, Tori, what are you going to do until then?"

"I'm going to get a dog."

Chapter Fourteen

"Whew, it sho' does stink in here!" Breathing through her mouth, Tori yelled out. "Hello? Anybody home?"

Footsteps came shuffling down the concrete hallway. The stench of tobacco reached her nostrils before she actually visualized the man. His uniform looked as if he'd either slept in it or took it out of a dryer after the spin cycle had finished, then slept in it that night, and wore it to work today. Evidently, he had lost his razor at some point because the stubble on his face had at least a three day start on the wrinkles in his clothing. No smile greeted her outstretched hand offered in greeting.

"Hi, my name is Victoria Stanfield and I'd like to see your dogs." Tori felt the tendons of her face contort into a grimace that she hoped passed for a smile.

His hand was cold, grainy, topped by nails yellowed by nicotine and seldom washed. Once he released his grasp, Tori resisted the urge to wipe her hand on her jeans.

"Name's Clarence Miller, Head Dog Catcher. What kinda dog you lookin' for?"

"I don't know, really. I 'spose I'll know when I find him or her."

Clarence let his gaze travel over her body and Tori felt dirtier than when she'd shaken hands with the slug.

"The dogs, Mr. Miller?"

"Oh yeah, you wanna see our collection of mangy mutts. Right this way. Watch out for the poop. My assistant's been out sick for a coupla days and the stuff is really piling up around here. If she don't come back tomorrow I'm gonna hafta fire her."

Tori could feel her fingernails pressing half-moon shapes into the palms of her hands. She was getting a headache from clinching her teeth so tightly together. She stayed several feet behind Clarence as he took them down another hall that led to loud barking. The closer they approached the dogs, the louder and more frantic their barks and whines became.

O Lord, the smell! I didn't know that the odor that lingered at the front door was only a prelude to the real assault. O God, these poor animals!

The stench she smelled was nothing compared to the way the spasms slammed against her ribs when she saw the dogs in their cages. Flies swarmed the area, settling onto the open sores that covered many of the animals. Green matter crusted over half-closed eyes in nearly half of the dogs. Both water and food dishes were empty. Small dogs and large dogs occupied the same cell, the smaller canine paying for that cruelty with their bodies. The feces was so plentiful that some of the dogs were lying in it. They had no choice; there was no room for all of them.

"Dear God in Heaven! Why are these dogs in this condition? What's wrong with you? Why isn't this place cleaned up and the dogs' wounds and infections medicated? I can't believe how horrible this is!"

"I told you I ain't had no help around here! They don't care if I have to do it all on my own. It ain't my fault. I do the best I can."

Tori ripped open her purse and pulled out her cell phone.

Clarence's eyes became enlarged and his attempt at a smile displayed long-neglected teeth, much the same way he neglected his job.

"Uh, who you calling, Missy? I'll take care of this mess and get their food out to 'em. I've just been overworked, ya know."

"I understand, Mr. Miller, and I'm going to get you some help right now. You poor man, having to do it all by yourself. We'll just take care of that lil' problem. Don't you worry, you'll get all you deserve."

Tori didn't try to soften her stony glare. Her call was answered within seconds.

"911. What's your emergency? Do you need an ambulance or police?"

"I need the police."

Clarence reached for her phone as he pleaded, "Please don't, Ma'am. I'll take care of them, I promise. Please don't do this to me!"

"Yes, send the police to 323 West Walker Street. Yes, the animal shelter." The word *shelter* was forced through clinched teeth. "Please, hurry. I'm afraid there's going to be a violent act committed any minute now."

Even Clarence's lips had turned gray. "I wouldn't hurt you, lady."

"I didn't say *you* were the one who was going to turn mean. Did I, Clarence?"

The officers arrived shortly and appeared justifiably appalled when they surveyed the grisly concrete and chain-link fenced squares. The first order of business was sliding the handcuffs on one Mr. Clarence Miller. A call was placed to the state headquarters to try, in vain, to give a description of what was going on, or rather, what wasn't going on. The head officer promised to have someone there within the hour.

Tori grabbed a long length of water hose with a pressure nozzle that was lying at the side of the building in plain view. When the policemen saw her spraying the animal habitats clean, they joined in her efforts. All the dogs were taken inside and, one by one, given food and water.

When a call came in saying that help would arrive within fifteen minutes, Tori decided to leave. Whoever came in to take over was going to have a madhouse to contend with, but at least it was clean and the dogs would be taken care of with the help of two area veterinarians.

As she was falling into the driver's seat, Tori stifled a scream when something touched her leg. Quickly pulling her legs into the car, she looked down to see a black and white dog gazing up at her. He placed one paw on the doorframe as if to ask her to not leave. Tori leaned over to stroke the dog's head.

"Hey there, boy! How'd you get out? Are ya on the lam? I've got an escaped jailbird, or maybe I should say escaped jail dog, on my hands, here. What're you doin', trying to hitch a ride out of here? You asking me to be your get-away driver, are ya?"

At her soft voice the dog jumped into her lap, having to mash his little fat butt in between Tori and the steering wheel. Once on her lap, he leaned against her chest and looked into her face with adoring eyes. It was Tori's undoing.

"Well, it looks like I got a dog, after all. I don't know if you're housebroken or not, but I guess I'll find out soon enough, won't I? How about... um, Max? You like that? Yeah, Max. That's a good name. Ready to go home, Max?"

Max was, indeed, ready to go home. He didn't even mind when Tori had to stop to buy him food and a collar. He seemed just as happy as he could be. The little Boston terrier didn't seem to mind anything now that he had a master to love.

Ah, Victoria is home! I hear her vehicle in the drive. What is that noise I hear? A dog? You have a dog, Victoria? And what manner of dog is this one? I've never seen such an animal. Black and white with streaks of red? I can already tell he's a feisty little guy.

Max ran into the house as if he had always belonged there. He began to sniff the carpet then abruptly stopped and ran to the corner of the room. He sat back on his haunches and cocked his head as he stared into the shadows. His tilted his head from side to side, a little frown between his big brown eyes. He'd periodically lift his bottom to shake his stub of a tail, then sit back down and appear to be listening to something.

"Who you visiting with, Max? Have you found my ghost that no human being could find? Tell him to be a good boy like you, Max, and stop scaring me."

Max, please tell your mistress it isn't my intention to frighten her. I'm here because she needs and wants me here. It is my fervent wish that she will soon be aware of my presence. For you see, I only want to love her.

Max turned his head around to look thoughtfully at Tori. His expression was so earnest, she felt that if he could, the dog would tell her something that would shake her very foundation.

Chapter Fifteen

It proved that her nerves were stretched as tight as a piano wire in that she dropped the screwdriver when the phone rang.

"Next thing you know, Max, I'm going to be hanging from the ceiling by my claws, I mean nails. Bet you'd like that, wouldn't you?" She found the phone beneath research notes she'd been reading when she decided to begin a new project.

"Hello, Lydia. How're they hanging?"

"At my age, pretty low unless I go get them lifted, my *young* author. What are you up to this fine, glorious day?"

"Fine and glorious day? Who is this and what did you do with Lydia?"

"Oh hush, Victoria. You can be such a brat sometimes. Now tell me, are you quite busy?"

"Well, I'm doing a bad impersonation of Bob Vila. I'm not a carpenter and I couldn't even play one on television."

"What in the world are you talking about, Tori? I swear there are times I truly think you've lost your mind."

"Don't doubt it, Lydia. I lost it years ago. Now to answer your question: I'm putting in a doggie door."

"A what? Why are you putting in a bloody doggie door?"

"Oh, just in case a rabid skunk may want to slip in to spend the night with me from time to time. I'm a gracious hostess for creatures large and small and word is spreading throughout the animal kingdom."

"Victoria Lynn..."

"Sheesh, I know when I'm in trouble. It's like having two mothers. I got a dog yesterday. Yes, a dog I said. But not before I got into a brawl at the animal shelter involving the cops and a few dozen of my closest canine friends. One of the dogs was wily enough to slip under the radar and make his escape. I helped him evade capture by secreting him away in my car. Yes, I know it was brash, foolish, probably detrimental to my future, but I don't care. I love him, I tell you!"

"O God, now what have you done, Tori?"

"Not a whole lot, really. My name may wind up in the newspaper, though. If you see it there, will you buy me a couple extra copies? You know, for Christmas cards and so forth. I have so many friends and relatives it's always hard to come up with a different card every holiday season."

Lydia's sigh spoke volumes. "I'm calling to say that your mother and I miss you and want to take you to dinner."

"Tonight? You want to go tonight?"

"No, I want to go next Tuesday, but I thought we could get in line tonight."

"As they said on Steel Magnolias, 'Spoken like a true smart-ass'. I like that about you, my British friend. I appreciate the offer but I think I'll pass. I need to spend time with Max."

"Who's Max?"

"My dog, Lydia. Haven't you been involved in the same conversation as I have?"

"I give up. If you change your mind, we'll be at the Outback at 7 P.M."

"Give Mom a hug for me and enjoy your meal. Smooch, smooch. Love ya, Lydia-poo."

"Hopelessly incorrigible. G'bye dear."

* * *

Because she wasn't home repair savvy, it took Tori over two hours to install the small door for her new friend. There was sawdust sprinkled around the opening and it coated nearby furniture.

"Oh dear, I should've put a sheet over the couch and tables. 'Sokay, I have a can of Pledge. And who cares? I honest to God put in a doggie door all by myself! And they said it couldn't be done! Who said it, you ask, Max? Why, they said it, that group of malcontents that are titled simply 'they'. No one knows who 'they' are, but 'they' are whispered about throughout all the land, in every level of society." She laughed at the dog's quizzical expression as he did his tilted head routine. "It was a great idea to adopt a dog. Now I have a reason to speak out loud."

For thirty minutes she worked on teaching Max how to use his very own doorway to the great bathroom outdoors. She went out on the porch, bent over and stuck her head in the door, calling for Max to come to her. After several attempts, Max understood her training but seemed to have trouble figuring out how to get back inside. Then Tori knelt on the carpet and stuck her head outside, getting wet dog kisses for her efforts. When Max at long last bounced back into the room, Tori praised him and rewarded him with a dog treat. She sat on the floor and smiled so hard her face hurt.

"Who's the smartest dog in the world? Max is, that's who! C'mere and let me hug you so tight you'll wiggle to get free."

It seemed like a great idea to Max who bounded across the room and jumped into Tori's arms. He caught her off-balance and she fell backward, her hand skidding beneath the recliner at her back. Her fingers came in contact with hard plastic. Leaning just a bit further to get a better grasp of the object, she juggled Max so he didn't slide off her lap.

He seemed as curious as she was when Tori pulled out the small black box. She laughed as Max sniffed the gadget because she had to gently push his nose away to find the buttons.

"Wow, it's one of those thingies the ghost busters had with them. What is it called? Oh crap, it's initials... E.V.P. thingamajig; that's it. A digital recorder. Let's rewind it and give it a twirl, Max. Let's see if my ghost decided to communicate, okay?"

Locating the rewind button, she nuzzled Max as she waited. She was still chuckling at his antics when she hit the "play" button. The contents of the instrument brought her laughter to a screeching halt.

"Max, please tell your mistress it isn't my intention to frighten her. I'm here because she needs and wants me here. It is my fervent wish that she will soon be aware of my presence. For you see, I only want to love her."

Unceremoniously dumping Max to the floor, Tori lunged to her feet. Still gripping the recorder, she grabbed her purse, scooped up the dog and ran out the door. Sharon was going to have company tonight. Tori hoped her mother would like Max.

She ran from the house like a woman searching for a nervous breakdown.

* * *

Avery held out his hand to her as she ran past him. "Victoria, wait! Please come back. I wish you weren't so terrified of me."

With his hand still held in front of him, Avery noticed that he could no longer see the door through a transparent palm. He raced to the mirror that hung on the back of Tori's bedroom door. Though not a totally solid form, he could see a dim outline of his body. He touched his own face and the man in the mirror duplicated his movements.

"As Victoria would say: 'holy crap!' "

Chapter Sixteen

Sharon and Lydia had been laughing when they saw Tori sitting on her mother's front porch. They continued to grin when they noticed Max with his head in Tori's lap as she smiled back at them.

Max put on quite a show when Sharon rubbed his tummy. He wriggled on his back and smiled at her.

"What a precious little dog, Tori! I didn't know he was a Boston terrier. What did you name him? Oh yeah, Max. Hello, Max. How're you doing, little guy? I'll bet you'll be spoiled rotten in no time flat."

Mother leaned over to kiss daughter and then frowned.

"What's wrong, Victoria?"

"I just thought we'd come by to see you. Let Max meet his grandmother."

Lydia squinted and pulled her mouth down in concentration.

"No, something's wrong. I can smell it, Tori."

"All you smell is what Max did in the yard. I'll get a garbage bag from the kitchen and clean it up. What's so funny? I heard you guys laughing when you got out of the car."

Lydia suddenly found the stars twinkling in the sky to be fascinating. Sharon began to chuckle.

"Don't let her innocent act fool you, Tori. That's all it is, an act. We got kicked out of the Outback."

Tori's mouth fell open.

"How in the world did you manage to get thrown out of a restaurant—Lydia?"

"She knows you too well, Lydia."

"Oh, they're just a bunch of bloody fools. I know when I'm intoxicated and this isn't one of those times."

Tori's heartbeat was starting to slow down to a more normal rhythm as she exchanged barbs with her agent.

"Good grief, you got so drunk you got pitched out in the street."

Lydia's face was crimson.

"We most certainly did NOT get pitched out into the street. What do you think it was, Tori, a lousy bar on Skid Row?"

"Doesn't matter what it was, YOU got thrown out of it! Lydia, do you ever think that maybe, just maybe, you drink too much?"

Sharon shook her head, silently asking Tori to cease and desist, that the teasing had gone too far this time.

"That's not funny, Tori. I'm not an alcoholic or a drunk. I can quit, I just don't want to right now."

"I'm just worried, Lydia. I love you and don't want anything bad to happen. Mom loves you, too. We both are trying to watch out for you."

"I can take care of myself, Victoria, so stop worrying. Sharon, shall we all go inside and have a nightcap?" Tori and Sharon, shaking their heads, followed Lydia as she strolled into the house.

Tori accepted her mother's offer of a glass of wine. Sharon's face registered her surprise.

"Alright, Tori, tell me what happened."

"I used to think it was endearing, the way you and Lydia seem to know me so well. Lately, I'm not so sure of that."

Lydia sat up straighter on her end of the couch.

"Yes, tell us, Victoria, just what is wrong. No more hem-hawing around."

"If I'm forced to tell you this, and I'm certain I will be, get comfortable, please close your mouths and open your minds. Buckle your seat belts 'cause it's going to be a bumpy ride."

Tori smiled at the similarities in these two women. Without plan or forethought, at the same moment, each of them removed their shoes and pulled their legs up to tuck their feet beneath themselves. They both settled into the cushions and looked at her expectantly.

"My house is haunted."

Sharon leaned forward. "Tori, honey, you know that isn't possible. There is no such thing as ghosts."

"This is preposterous. As your agent I appreciate the fact that you have a vivid, active imagination, but surely you don't truly believe in ghosts. What's next, Tori, a troll under your bed?"

"Oh gee, that's so funny, let me write it down so I won't forget it. Lydia, it's true, and I have proof."

Tori told them about all the strange phenomena that had been happening in the house. She went into detail about the parapsychologists and all their equipment, ending it by saying the group had found nothing that was certain. They'd suggested she find someone to channel, a medium of sorts, to bring out the dead—if they did, in fact, inhabit the house.

Lydia snorted disdainfully. "You're not going to do that, are you, Victoria?"

"I don't know, I just might after what I found this evening. While playing around with Max I stumbled across a piece of the ghost busters' equipment. It's a digital recorder used for what they call E.V.P—electronic voice phenomena."

Sharon paled. "You have something on tape?"

"Not tape, but yes, I have something. Here, listen."

Max, please tell your mistress it isn't my intention to frighten her. I'm here because she needs and wants me here. It is my fervent wish that she will soon be aware of my presence. For you see, I only want to love her.

Sharon shuddered and Lydia cursed, then attempted to find a logical explanation.

"It must've been one of those weird people, the ghost hunters, whatever. They left you a message so that when you found it you'd call them back and they could get more money out of you."

"Two things wrong with that theory, Lydia. First, they don't charge for their services. Second, I didn't get Max for a few of days after they left, so they couldn't have been speaking to him on the recorder. Anyway, this voice has a slight accent, one I can't identify, and none of the men in that group spoke with one. I would've remembered if they had."

For the next two hours they tried to figure out just what it all meant. Just after midnight they called an end to the discussion after coming to no conclusions.

Sharon asked Lydia to spend the night because the agent was too unsteady on her feet to drive. Tori joined her mother in insisting Lydia stay there. The feisty Brit decided she'd had enough of their smothering mothering, as she called it, and left in a flurry of perfume and wine-scented aroma.

Tori took Max out for a short walk down the block. She locked the door behind her when she came back in. She didn't wait for an invitation to spend the night—she had no intention of going home tonight.

* * *

Tori came to the conclusion that her agent rarely slept and that she took great pleasure in jolting her awake at all ungodly hours of the morning. Lydia was back again. This time she burst into the guestroom, pulling on Sharon's sleeve as she tugged her into the room with her. When she heard them, Tori squinted her eyes against the bright sunlight as Lydia threw the drapes open.

"Wake up, Victoria Lynn Stanfield! Today is a glorious day, a special day, your lucky day!"

"Have you already been drinking this morning, Lydia? Why can't you just visit without fanfare and blaring wind instruments? Is it too much to ask that you wait until a reasonable hour to blast someone awake? What's all the hub-bub about this time?"

Lydia looked at Sharon in mock shock. "This time? Did she say 'this time'? You'd think this happens all the time. You'd think that it's every day that Miss Stanfield gets a contract for an embarrassing amount of money from a New York publisher. You'd think that Miss Stanfield is accustomed to receiving an advance check of the upper end of five figures. And you'd think the brat would show some gratitude!"

Any lingering vestiges of sleep vanished. Tori threw the blankets back and scrabbled to her feet in a jumble of clothing she'd dropped beside the bed the night before, causing her to fall on top of Max. When she disentangled herself, the dog sat up and looked at her as if she'd lost her mind.

"Contract? Publisher? Five figures? Upper end of five figures? O God, tell me what happened, Lydia!"

Sharon threw her arms around her daughter, happy tears streaming down her face. "Oh honey, I'm so happy for you, so proud of you! You've worked very hard for this."

Tori lifted her mother off her feet and twirled her around the room before dropping her onto the bed. While jumbled together, they both grabbed Lydia to pull her onto the bed with them. The room was filled with laughter and tears of joy.

Sharon was the first one up, as always, ready to be the perfect hostess.

"Come on! Let's go drink a cup of tea!"

Tori hugged her agent one more time.

"For this even I'll drink a cup of tea. But you have to tell me everything, Lydia. Hurry! I can't wait another second!"

Lydia began explaining as Sharon put the tea kettle on to heat.

"I know that you're still working on the new book and that you've been pushing yourself hard to complete it by deadline. But I was going through some old manuscripts in my office and came across two of your earlier novels. You didn't think they were marketable. Even though I disagreed, we shelved them. Then I thought, 'We've got a publisher who has read some of her work and likes it enough to want to see the completed book so why not show him something else while we've got his attention?' I didn't tell you because you seem to be a nervous wreck lately."

Tori grinned, unable to work up any hurt over the remark.

"So I just waited to see what he had to say. He called me at five this morning. And you think I get you up early? He said that even though the two books had nothing to do with the Avery Norcross line, he's still very interested. He faxed a contract with an offer and I've tentatively accepted his terms. All we need now is for you to go over the contract and sign if you're happy with it."

"What about the current book? Is he still interested in it, too?"

"That's the lovely part. Yes, he still wants it, in addition to the other two. I think you've arrived, Tori."

Sharon began to cry in earnest as she set the cups of tea on the table.

"You did it, baby. Finally, finally, you did it. Just as I always knew you would. Congratulations, Honey."

Lydia patted Tori's hand and smiled.

"Today will be a day of celebration. A girls' day out, doing whatever comes to mind. Let's start with brunch, shall we? Let's try that new restaurant down on Riverside. My treat!"

* * *

After a meal that left them moaning with too-full bellies, the trio headed for Utica Square to "ooh" and "ahh" over the classy clothing at Miss Tatiana's and Fifth Avenue. Lydia bought a lovely semi-formal dress to wear for a cocktail party she was certain would be held in Tori's honor once the books were released. With a great deal of cajoling, she convinced the other two women to purchase outfits for the same occasion.

Sharon's tea-length dress was a rich crème color accentuated with rose pink trim. She blushed when both Tori and Lydia told her how flattering the dress was to her.

"I'll need to get my hair cut and I think I'll finally have my nails done. I've never done that but if my baby is going to be famous, I'll have to take better care of my appearance."

"Mom, I can't believe you said that. You're always beautiful, even in house shoes and that ratty old bathrobe you love so much."

"You're such a sweet daughter. Now, let's find an outfit for Miss Victoria Stanfield. What d'ya think, Lydia? Blue for my auburn-haired child?"

"Oh no, she should wear green. A deep, jade green would complement Tori's coloring beautifully. Find a saleslady and tell her we'll accept nothing less than glamorous for our talented author."

It only took eleven dresses for all three women to decide that Tori wasn't going to find what Sharon and Lydia were looking for her to wear. They were able to come to some sort of uneasy settlement on a beautiful trouser suit. Lydia said that it would look fine for a less-austere event than a cocktail party, and she was certain they'd find just the right dress, eventually.

"You two act as if this were a debutante ball, a coming-out party. We don't even know if there will BE such an affair. Yet here we are, buying clothes with price tags so extravagant they make me gasp."

The agent chuckled. "It won't be long before you won't even bother looking at a price tag, Tori. How about catching a movie or let's drop by one of the comedy clubs?"

They couldn't decide which movie to watch so they wound up at The Laugh Track. It was a full house and everyone was laughing in all the right places. Lydia seemed to feel she had to support the national liquor distributors so she bought drink after drink, toasting Tori with increasing praise which each new round.

Sharon had switched to coffee after a couple of mixed drinks. Tori drank only Coke because she didn't like the taste of alcohol. Because of their sobriety, Lydia's drinking was more noticeable than usual when she began to guffaw at the comedians on stage. Tori and Sharen knew that, had she been sober, Lydia would never have allowed herself to sound so coarse.

When the server came back around, Tori caught her eye and shook her head, trying to signal her to keep walking before Lydia could order another drink. The lady saw her gestures and understood. When Lydia stopped her to order another whiskey sour, the waitress refused to serve her any longer. And that's when it got ugly.

"Just who the hell do you think you are, anyway? You stupid lil' twit! Where's your manager? I demand to speak to your boss, immediately!"

Heads turned in their direction, shushing noises were tossed at them from every corner of the club and it all served to inflame Lydia to a fever-hot explosion. Tori and Sharon both saw it coming and grabbed the Brit's arms, pulling her from the building.

"Bloody hell! Get your hands off me this instant! I will not be treated…"

Sharon's voice was low and steady. "Shut up, Lydia. You're about one slurred epitaph away from jail."

Never let it be said that the mother and daughter team didn't work together for the betterment of world peace. Tori's voice was a subdued as her mother's.

"Lydia, you're belligerent, out of control. You'll regret this tomorrow. Now, let's go before the management decides to make an example of you."

Shrill and ear-splitting, "An example? I just wish they'd try… Who're you calling, Tori?"

"I'm calling a cab, Lydia. You're in no condition to drive Mom home."

Sharon smiled at her. "It's okay, honey. I'll drive her to my house and she can spend the night. She can nurse a hangover at my house in the morning, as well as her own. Do you want us to drop you off at your car? Did you park close by?"

"No thanks, Mom. I'm just right over here. It'll be fine. Lydia, don't even try to drive that house on wheels you call a Lincoln. Let Mom drive."

"This is ludicrous! I'm perfectly capable of driving my own damned car, Miss Stanfield! But just to appease you and your dear mum, I'll give her the keys."

"Alright Lydia. I need to stop by a store so I'll see you at Mom's in just a little bit. I have to come by and pick up Max. Mom, drive carefully."

"Absolutely! See you in a few, Baby Girl. Love you."

Tori smiled at her mother. "I love you, too, Mom."

As she was walking away to her own car, Tori heard a commotion behind her. She turned just in time to see Lydia leap behind the wheel of her car and Sharon scrambling around the other side to jump in before the car began to roll forward.

Tori began to run toward the big black monster with every intention of dragging Lydia from behind the wheel, but the car shot out of the parking lot, tires squealing.

She sighed in frustration and crossed her fingers that her agent didn't take out anybody's mail box along the road leading to her mother's house.

Even though she had spent more time than she thought she would at the store, Tori got to her mother's house before the other two women. She sat in the car a few minutes but decided to go on in when she heard her dog barking. She fished her mother's extra key out of her purse and went inside to wait.

Max greeted her with enthusiasm bordering on mania. The great thing about having a dog is you always have someone happy to see you, grateful that you're home at last.

When the two older women hadn't shown up thirty minutes later, Tori figured Lydia had strong-armed Sharon into either stopping by a liquor store, or worse, another club. She'd wait a little longer, then leave and call them again when she got home.

"Wanna go for a short walk, Max? Please tell me you didn't have an accident somewhere in my mom's house. No, don't tell me. If you spoke to me it'd be the last thing I need to knock me over the edge. Are you smilin' at me? You think that's funny, do you? Let me grab your leash and we'll hit the sidewalk."

Max began to jump up and down, tongue flopping out of his grinning mouth and barking little yips of happiness when he saw his neon blue leash.

"No matter what, Max, you can always make me laugh."

The skies had turned a vicious leaden color. She glanced upward and remembered hearing about the threat of rocky weather.

"C'mon Max, do your thing. We need to get back inside before this storm hits. Hurry Buddy, pee!"

A gust of wind raced past her, blowing her hair over her head, covering her face.

"Max, either you do it soon or forever hold your pee."

A small funnel of wind, a dust devil, screamed into them and nearly pushed Tori into the tree that Max had finally decided was his spot. Living in Oklahoma makes you sit up and take notice of *anything* that resembles a *funnel* of wind, even if it's a small one. After all, the big tornadoes begin with a small funnel.

"Okay, that's it, Bubba. I hope you got it out of your system 'cause you're headed back to the house with me—now. I love you but I ain't gettin' blown away for you."

It only took half the time to make the journey back inside Sharon's house. It helped when Tori had a strong wind at her back, pushing her along. It's as if Mother Nature was saying, "Get inside. Hurry up now—go!"

Tori grabbed the silver tea kettle from the stove and filled it with water. As she waited for it to heat, she filled Max's food and water dishes. Max showed his appreciation with a head rub against her leg.

In the bedroom, Tori took a pair of faded jeans out of a dresser drawer. She kept some of her old clothes at her mom's just for occasions like this so she never had to bring anything with her if she spent the night. She smiled when the bright beams of headlights flashed across the window. She tugged on her tennis shoes as fast as she could, wanting to be at the door to open it so her mom wouldn't have to use her key.

Tori opened the door with a flourish, a big goofy smile on her face.

"It's about time! I put on the tea..."

He was a large man with a receding hairline generously peppered with gray. He held his hat in his hands, unconsciously turning it in circles. Tori's gaze traveled from the silver badge over his heart to the sadness in his blue eyes.

"Good evenin', Ma'am. Are you Victoria Stanfield?"

Her heartbeat accelerated and suddenly she had trouble breathing due to the anvil sitting on her chest.

"Yes."

"Mizz Stanfield, I'm sorry to have to tell you this..."

Tori took a step back, nearly stepping on Max who was curiously silent as he, too, stared at the stranger. She heard, as well as saw, the neighbor's trash can rattle down the street. She noticed that trees and neighboring houses faded into an encroaching sheet of tears.

It seemed the only thing she could do was shake her head.

"No... no."

"Ma'am? Uh, Victoria? I'm so sorry. There was an accident..."

Tori held her hand up in self-defense against the words the state trooper was determined to say. He continued in a hesitant tone.

"Lydia Sommers and your mother were involved in a collision with a tractor-trailer rig out on the expressway, near the Utica exit."

Tori couldn't speak. She prayed he would stop.

"The driver of the truck sustained only a few scrapes and bruises, but the ladies..."

She managed to hitch a breath.

"How bad is it?"

"It's bad, Miz Stanfield."

Tori felt as if she'd slipped into a dream state, an alternate universe where nothing could ever hurt her.

"By 'bad', do you mean they're terribly injured?"

With a sad look, he acknowledged the prophetic confirmation of her worst fear written across her pale face.

"No, honey, I mean it's as bad as it gets."

The voice she heard felt as if it came from someone else's vocal cords, spoken through an ethereal being's lips.

A frozen spear of pain greater than she'd ever known pierced her heart.

"Which one is dead?"

A part of her brain argued this was all a lie, but her heart began to contract with the acceptance of the truth. But hope is a strong emotion, hard to let go of.

"I'm so sorry, Honey. It's both of them. Both of them are dead."

The wind came to an abrupt halt, dropping its cargo on the ground. In the kitchen the tea kettle released the sound of an anguished scream, the way that Tori could not. The officer's face blurred in her vision because of her tears before her sobs matured into wails of heartbreak.

* * *

It was a robot that extinguished all the lights in Sharon's house and locked the door behind itself. Even the dog who was usually so excited at being outside that he'd run everywhere at full tilt, walked slowly with his mistress to her car.

Max rested his chin on her knee as Tori drove home. She didn't even sense him staring up at her with sad brown eyes. Nor did she notice a dim light burning when she pulled into her driveway. A light she had not left on when she ran from the building in a fear she no longer felt. This emptiness, this blank canvas, this nothingness where you go when all hope is gone.

She held the door open for the dog then walked in behind him. Once again, she almost ran into his solid little body parked in her way. She frowned as she glared at him until she noticed he was staring with great concentration at the other side of the room.

It seemed to take an hour for her to turn her head so that she was facing the far wall. When her eyes reached the same sight Max was seeing, Tori's knees turned to water. Just like that, she was brought back to reality when a needle of terror pierced her brain.

Her throat spasmed in fear and her stomach twisted into a knot of terror. Despite the chill in the air, she began to sweat. Clinching her teeth, she willed her body to move one foot backward. She tried to scream but could only force out a pitiful mewling, like an injured cat. An involuntary shudder passed through her.

Is this some sort of grief-induced hallucination or dementia?

Wisps of mist sailed across the floor punctuated by a soft glow that pulsed in counterpoint to her terrified heartbeat. Was it something too horrible to truly contemplate? Again, she told her limbs to move and again they refused. Then she heard him. The hair on the back of her neck rose in a fear as cold and deep as the Arctic Ocean. She knew within the space of a heartbeat that she was not alone. She saw the shape sharpen and take a more distinct form of a tall, dark man, and he stepped out of the mist, toward her. There was a sense of anticipation, an urgent expectancy of something or *someone*, wishing for her in her darkest hour.

Tori stared at him, compelled to watch him, as unable to look away as changing the ebb and flow of the tides. Even though her mind processed the image, informed her she was correct in what she was seeing, her heart stuttered, skipping several beats, threatening to stop if the man advanced closer to her.

Her gaze began at the top of his head, to his hair that brushed against the raised collar of his shirt, to the ice-blue eyes, down his patrician nose to his sculptured lips, parting into a smile that showcased his brilliant teeth. Downward to the wide shoulders, narrow hips and *O God, don't let your eyes linger there!* to his muscled thighs, to the stockings covering his perfectly formed muscled calves, ending at the buckled shoes on his feet.

He was more handsome than even her imagination could have designed. His jet black hair shined blue in the light of the lamp and the compassion in his eyes did not detract from their beauty. He held his strong arms out to her, beseeching her to walk into his embrace.

Am I no longer able to separate reality from fantasy?

True, he seemed to lack the substance of a real, flesh and blood man. In the briefest flicker, he faded. She wished she'd at least seen a serpentine of smoke, as she imagined a ghost would appear, instead of "it" just simply vanishing like that. First it was there, the next it was gone. It didn't fade or walk through a wall—it was just GONE.

Certain she had misinterpreted her own eyesight, she stepped backward, closer to the door. Then she realized the form, or whatever it was, hadn't completely left.

What is this? Is this some sort of illusion lurking within a reality?

Just as placing an undeveloped photo into a pan of developer brings forth a picture, the man's image became more solid, more detailed. It was as if someone had dialed up a rheostat and the apparition began to form into the shape of a man. He slowly, surely, without question, materialized into...

It's his eyes. That's how I know. That's why I'm certain. But ohmygod, this isn't possible. It's insane! But those eyes, and the expression that I have mentally visualized thousands of times tells me that this is truly, inexplicably, undeniably HIM.

As she realized she could no longer see the wall behind him, Tori began to become light-headed.

He was luminous and she felt compelled to stare at him. His returning expression one of... love? His eyes held her hostage.

What's next? Do I start believing in vampires and werewolves? Anything that goes bump in the night?

She had envisioned his eyes as the pure blue of the Arctic Ocean, but the sultriness there raised the temperature of the room.

He reached out his hand and the touch was so precise that it couldn't be the wind, especially when no windows were open. Her astonishment and fear deepened into awe. Though still doubting her own sanity, her pulse settled into a fast rhythm and her head began to clear, but then he spoke.

"Victoria, my darling. Let me hold you and perhaps lighten the heavy burden upon your loving heart."

She never heard or felt the soft thud as her body hit the carpet.

Chapter Seventeen

She didn't immediately open her eyes when she awoke. Through the haze of the state between waking and sleeping, Tori had a nagging feeling that something was wrong, that something horrible had happened. Then it all came back to her in a flood of torment. She bit her lip and squeezed her eyes shut as tightly as possible, trying to force the nightmare sights and sounds from her memory.

The blankets were smothering, but she couldn't make herself pull them from her head. When she felt a weight settle onto the side of the bed and gentle hands tugging at the confining cover, she suddenly remembered another shocking event of last night.

Inch by miniscule inch, Tori began to pull her head free of its confines. When the blanket reached her eyebrows, she stared with large, rounded green eyes as she jerked the comforter off her head. She knew her hair was wild and her mouth hung open but she wasn't cognizant to the point she could correct those problems.

It appeared that she'd lost the power of speech, also. It didn't help that he sat there, that amazing smile lighting up his face. He leaned forward to cup her face in his hands. Tori jerked away so hard she slammed the back of her head against the headboard. At once she reclaimed the power of speech.

"Ouch! Man, that's gonna leave a mark!"

"Good morning, Victoria."

His voice not only sounded familiar, it felt so gloriously right saying her name.

"Who are you? What are you doing in my house?"

"Darling, you know who I am."

"This is not possible. No way, no how, nun-uh."

"Yes, my love, it is, indeed, possible. It must be for I am here, am I not?"

"You are what I've felt, the thing that Max stares at. Oh! The one that knocks my things to the floor!"

"I apologize for that, darling. I was only trying to garner your attention."

"How did you get here? O God, I can't believe I'm talking to you. You're not real and I'm crazy."

"You are not crazy and I am real. At least I think I'm real. It's so difficult to know, really."

"What do you mean you don't know? How the hell can you not know whether or not you're real?"

"Well Victoria, you must admit this is an unusual set of circumstances, true?"

"Well—yeah."

"I can only tell you how I came to be, at least in my own opinion. You may, perhaps, help me to better understand how it... I, came to be, here and now."

She had to get away, had to think, and she couldn't do that with him so close.

"Wait, I have to go to the bathroom. You know how it is when you first wake up... or maybe you don't."

I don't know because I have no idea how close to human you could possibly be.

She cast her eyes sideways at him, pulling free of the blankets, tugging at her t-shirt, hotly aware of how her body reacted to the cold morning air in the bedroom. She crossed her arms across her chest and turned to slip past him. Her feet brushed against the side of his leg and she felt his calf muscle tense as her foot grazed him.

Nothing diaphanous there; it felt solid, real—manly.

"Well, I guess I should be grateful I still have all my clothes on."

The look of utter shock on his chiseled face would have been funny if the entire situation wasn't something straight out of an episode of The Twilight Zone.

"Victoria! I can't believe you'd even consider that I'd..."

"Oh, keep your pantaloons on, I was kidding. It's something I do when I'm nervous or scared."

"Madame, I assure you, I don't wear pantaloons."

Tori touched the power button on a small radio she kept on top of her dresser. He may not like the sound of the music, but the bathroom was just on the other side of the thin wall separating it from her bedroom.

The tragic loss of the night before threatened to assault her heart, which would have crippled her to the point of unreasonableness. She took several deep breaths, promised herself she'd allow herself to deal with it later. She then blushed as she flushed, washed her hands, and walked quickly to the kitchen to lean against the wall, gulping air.

What the crap is going on here? Am I no longer able to separate reality from fantasy? Have I finally, at long last, checked into the Rubber Ramada where all the mattresses are nailed to the walls? It's simply impossible that a fictional man, one created in my imagination, has been skulking in the background, then stepped through the shadows, slowly taking solid form! O God, I wonder if I can find a therapist who will take me in immediately.

She pulled a knife from the butcher block on the counter, held it at her side as she walked back into the bedroom. Bobby Darin's hit "Dream Lover" was playing on the radio and she found Avery grinning at her as he listened to the song.

"I remember the night you sang this while you were holding some sort of brown paper tube in your hand..."

She raised an eyebrow at him and killed the power of the radio as she came back into the room.

Okay, I have enough to worry about to not remember that I was probably singing right before I got into the tub, which means I was nude. O God...

She nestled in the middle of the bed, knees bent, and legs across each other.

"Okay, tell me."

Avery took her hand in his and Tori quickly pulled free of his grasp.

"Don't touch me. Just tell me."

He smiled and the deep dimples at his cheek elicited a small gasp before she caught it.

Yeah, there ya go, Stupid. Let him know that you'd like to kiss those dimples and...

"Why do you smile so damned much? I don't have anything to smile about and you're getting on my last nerve. So tell me how you came 'to be.' "

Even though he'd dropped the smile and no longer held her hand, his pull was strong, magical.

"For you are the magnet and I am the steel." Oh, for the love of Pete, Tori, stop thinking in song titles!

"I've seen you for many months. Not in the way that I see you now, but as if through a deep fog. At first it frightened me, as you can well imagine. I thought you were either a witch, a demon, or a goddess, and I didn't want to truly find out which.

"I could see your face only, then slowly I could see the rest of your body, walking through the mist. After a bit I could make out some of your speech, some of it hard for me to understand, to know the meaning of it.

"Then you began to come closer, so close I could touch you, or the ghost of you. But whenever you saw me or felt me near you, you ran in fear. I regretted that for all I wanted to do was speak to you, to wipe the tears from your eyes.

"All of a sudden, for some reason, I began to be drawn here, to your world, your time. What I'd felt when I first saw your countenance was nothing compared to the fear I experienced when I came to *this* place." He gestured with his hand to illustrate the room, the house, the world. "I was filled with wonder and terror."

"Just like that, you popped into this world? For some weird reason you simply can't fathom, you busted into this time frame—without knowing how you got here?"

"Yes, that *is* what I am saying."

"You don't recognize sarcasm, do you?"

His face was confused, his eyebrows surprised peaks on his forehead.

"Oh, Avery, that's impossible. That is, if Avery is really your name."

"What other name would I have, other than the one you gave me?"

Tori's epiphany was obvious on her face.

"You're the one who wrote those chapters of the book!"

A bright red crept over his face and he cast his eyes downward, the long dark lashes feathering against his cheeks.

"Yes, it was I. It wasn't too difficult to work that machine after I watched you do so for several days. You are a good teacher."

Tori's jaw muscles were clinched so hard her words came out through her teeth.

"I had no idea I was teaching anyone anything. You actually stood behind me as I worked, you..."

Her eyes once again glared open.

"You've been there when I slept, when I took a shower, when I changed my clothes! O my God, you've seen everything, you bastard!"

Avery's hands were moving frantically, his head shaking his negative response, his words pleading with Tori to please stop and listen to him.

"A gentleman would never do what you suggest I've done, Victoria!"

"Avery, hello! As you said, I created you and I know I made you a cad, a womanizer. I *know* what you are."

"No Victoria. That is *your* concept of my character but it's an untrue one. Now that I've gained solidity I make my own decisions, and I've decided I don't much care for the character you created for me."

"Are you honestly trying to tell me that you're your own man now, in this time, in this world?"

"That is exactly what I'm telling you. Here and now, I am a gentleman."

"Oh really? And pray tell, what other sentiments do you have to add?"

"I love you, Victoria. That is my only other sentiment."

"Avery, that's preposterous. You're a fictional person, you don't exist other than on the pages of a book!"

"How can you stand there, Victoria, look at me, and say that? Am I not solid? Can you not hear my voice, smell my scent...?"

Tori closed her eyes and inhaled deeply. The scent of him was heady and sexy.

He stepped closer and looked into her eyes. She saw the raw desire there. His lips claimed hers and Tori became faint with the feelings that kiss evoked. He released her lips and smiled into her eyes.

"Does not that kiss feel real to you, my love?"

When she could take a deep breath Tori frowned at him.

"Okay, granted I don't know what's going on here but I'll eventually figure it out. If you're not a full-blown apparition, you're still... paranormal. So, until then, no terms of endearment and absolutely no physical contact of any kind!"

"I have a theory, if you'd like to hear it, my... Victoria."

Her sigh was deep and ragged.

"Sure, let's talk it out. Maybe that's the only way we'll figure out the most mystifying thing that's ever happened to me in my life."

"It might be best, Victoria, if you would let me tell you, without interruption, how I feel this has happened. We can... how do they say that... rap about it when I'm done."

Victoria couldn't stop the grin that refused to be denied.

"Rap about it? You've been watching too much TV."

A frown drew his eyebrows together.

"TV? What is that?"

Tori pointed to the television set across the room.

"Oh! The box with so many different people in it! I haven't figured that one out just yet. I have so many questions, and not just about the... TV. But, please, tell me one thing, Victoria. Where do all those people go when you turn off the box? I've been so worried about them. They're all so small that I don't see how they can possibly take care of themselves. At first I was so concerned I couldn't sleep but then when I watched the box the next day, there all of them were again, and they seemed to be fine. And why do these little women on TV behave so badly? Every day they have another man..." the blush rose from his collar to his forehead, "I just don't understand so many things."

"O Lord, you've been watching soap operas. No wonder you're confused." Tori began to chuckle and then laughed out loud before she could reel it in. "Avery, we have so many problems to work out. Let's discuss TV, the little people on it, and scantily clad women later, okay?"

The laughter dried on her lips when she realized her amusement at his expense hurt him.

"I have a feeling this is going to be an epic story, the telling of your trip to this era. Why don't I make us some coffee before we start?"

"Coffee? That's very kind of you, but do you happen to have any tea?"

Tears jumped to the surface. "You stubborn Brits!" Then she smiled at him to take the sting from her words.

* * *

Avery settled himself into the cushions on the other side of the sofa. His heartbeat had slowed down to a frantic rhythm instead of galloping along at top speed, but all it took to get out of control was for Victoria to come back into the room. He wasn't sure how this all came about, how he was now able to be seen and heard by her, he only knew he was so happy it had finally happened.

Victoria's expression was one of expectation and Avery realized she was waiting for him to begin. He forced himself to take a deep breath, made his body appear to be relaxed, and carefully placed his tea cup on the table so that he wouldn't be betrayed by his trembling hands. He took a deep breath then smiled at her.

"It must have been nearly two years ago when I noticed I was... changing, for want of a better word. In the beginning it was a bit unsettling when I would seem to *black out*. That was a term I learned from your TV. I would seem to wake up without ever having realized I was asleep. At first it was for short periods of time, mere minutes. These spells were to become longer in duration as the months passed.

"When I awoke I had a vague feeling that I had been speaking to someone I didn't know, at times and in places I wasn't familiar with. It began to happen with more and more frequency and with each episode the mist would lighten as if the sun were burning it away, and your image would come into focus. Then it became progressively clearer until not only could I plainly see the woman I was trying to speak to, but I could remember every detail of her face when I came back to my senses.

"I grew pallid, so much so that not only was my mother worried, even the villagers expressed concern. At times, I felt weak and out of touch with my body. Then I started fading, truly unable to see my own fingers, then my arms! I was terrified until I realized I could still utilize those extremities, though they were invisible. But it didn't stop there. There were instances where half my body was translucent. I had to come up with reasons to be away from the village during those times. Had any of the townspeople seen me in that form, not only would it have terrorized them, they would have burned me at the stake!

"Only when you were out of this house could I go back to my land, my time. It was your presence that anchored me to you, to this world. And only when you were sleeping could I write the words that would bring you to me, through the shadows, into the mist, where I waited on the other side, wherever or whatever that place was."

"Your life, your other relationships—none of that was real in your world?"

His handsome face took on a bright shade of pink. "Yes, Tori, they were real. At least to me they felt as real as I'm sure your life is to you. You're a wonderful writer and your description of me, my family, my home—you made it all real."

Tori clicked the ends of her thumb nails together. "The women...?"

"As I said, Victoria, I loathed the character you created for me. It's why I changed it as soon as possible."

"Is that why you began writing entire chapters in my book?"

"Certainly because of that but also because my beloved mother was dying and I wanted to ensure I would be by her side when it happened."

Physical pain struck at Tori's heart when she remembered the night before; the last time she saw her mother, Lydia, the wreck, the police officer standing there twisting his hat in his hand...

"I'm so sorry, Avery. O God, I'm so sorry I did that to you, hurt you that much!" She began to cry. Avery moved closer and put his arms around her.

"To everything there is a season, my love. Our mothers' seasons have ended."

Tori sighed deeply. "Ecclesiastes 3."

Avery pulled back to look questioningly into her eyes. "No, The Byrds, 1965."

Tori pulled out of his arms and bent at the waist, laughing so hard she nearly lost her breath. When she could again breathe normally, she wiped the tears, both sad and funny, from her cheeks.

"Now there's something that I didn't expect. That's my favorite decade of music but how did you know that song?"

"I heard it on that box with the flashing lights that you kicked when I took away its power, to get your attention. I like that song."

Even though she was still smiling, a crease between eyes illustrated her confusion.

"I wonder if you're merely a visitor here from another realm, brought here by my longing and imagination. Could this be some sort of early onset of dementia?"

Avery reached out and slowly took her hand and placed her palm against his chest.

"Do you not feel a heartbeat? Can you not feel the rhythm of my breathing?" Removing her hand he titled his head and kissed the palm, then kept a firm, but nonthreatening grip, so that Tori could not pull away. "Did you not just feel my lips upon your skin?"

She could feel her own heartbeat picking up speed.

"Yes, all of that's true, real, but it doesn't explain what's happened."

"Victoria, does it not seem as if each time something hurts you, you've sensed me in the background?"

"Yes! All the more reason to believe I'm having some sort of breakdown. I mean, my world starts falling apart, piece by piece, and each time a chunk crumbles, you seemed to become more solid, more real."

"It took a great deal of energy and thought to make that happen, Victoria. I just wanted you to realize you're not alone, that someone who loves you above all others is here, just waiting for you to acknowledge that presence."

"But... why?"

"Have you not loved me since the first novel?"

She knew the longing on her face gave her away and Tori did nothing to hide it.

Avery pulled her back into his arms.

"Yes, as I have loved you all this time. You were worth fighting for, Victoria."

She sank to the floor, tears coursing down her cheeks. Avery knelt, put his hands on her shoulders and helped her to stand. He then wrapped her in his arms and they both swayed from the emotions juggernauting through their bodies. He put a finger beneath her chin to lift her tear-stained face and began to kiss the tears away. With each contact his lips made with her skin, the more ardent his embrace became. When he could stand no more, he leaned down, tilted his head, and placed his lips over hers.

At first gentle, the kiss grew in both temperament and pressure until it took on a life of its own. Avery tightened his lips just enough to pull Tori's mouth further into his, then he gently ran his tongue across her puckered lips. With a deep, quivering sigh, Tori opened her lips and they were both consumed.

Tori, who had lost her husband, mother, and agent who had been her best friend, who felt as if her life had hit rock bottom, was at long last home.

Chapter Eighteen

Tori disentangled herself from the sheets so she could look into Avery's eyes. She had a question she dreaded to ask, but she had to have an answer. It would determine how she lived the rest of her life.

"Avery?"

His slow, sensual smile and half-closed eyelids nearly derailed her, making her want to throw the sheets on the floor and leave the worry about the future for later. She took a deep breath and Avery's eyes widened in appreciation at the way her chest lifted the sheet. He turned enough to lean on an elbow and moved his face closer, closer...

"No wait! If you do that I'll never be able to think and get this out. I have a very important question and I want you to consider all the possible angles before you answer me. Okay? We got a deal?" She stuck out her right hand.

Avery gently took her hand in both of his and began to run his tongue down the length of her lifeline.

"Avery!" She pulled her hand free. "You have got to stop doing that or we'll never get anything done."

He sat up more, the sheet sliding down to his hips, barely covering his obvious burgeoning desire. At the moment, all Tori could think about was how happy she was she'd created him to be so... manly.

"We could get much done, my Beloved, if you'd just drop the sheet, lie back and..."

"Avery, I am warning you!"

He pulled on a good impression of a chastised little boy, tugged the sheet up to his neck, and leaned against the headboard, as if awaiting further orders.

"Yes, Miss Stanfield?"

Tori fought to hide the grin but he saw it and returned it sevenfold.

"Avery, what are you going to do?"

"Do? Do about what?"

Tori steeled her nerves, forced herself to smile, and asked her question:

"Are you going to stay here, in this era, with me—or are you going to go back?"

He brushed the back of his fingers across her cheek and looked into her eyes.

"I have nothing to go back to. My mother is gone and the villagers believe me to be dead. All I would truly miss would be Mankala. When I began to feel that there would be a day I would fade from that world into this, I found someone to love and care for Mankala as well as I did, so I know he is in kind hands."

Tori grabbed his face in both her hands and began to kiss him, smiling into his eyes.

Chapter Nineteen

Victoria sat beside the huge stone fireplace, a red shawl wrapped around her shoulders. Beside her some of the women from town had gathered to discuss their latest book club selection. The room was bathed in a soft glow from the fire and the friendship.

Tori was grateful that Avery had convinced her to make this a working farm with everything that entailed. There were chickens, cows, a few pigs, and horses. Lots of horses. The year before she had bought her husband a gift that he treasured; a beautiful chestnut Arabian horse he immediately name Mankala. And with the money her mother and agent left her, along with the steady stream of income from the books, they could afford a lot of help. Tori loved the animals although milking cows wasn't her strong suit.

She also appreciated that Avery had gently, slowly but surely, insinuated her into the life of the nearby town. As a loner, she'd never felt the need to be in the company of others but Avery was an extrovert, filled with kindness and love that he had to share or explode. Not even Tori had the capacity to hold all the love her husband had to offer. The thought made her smile.

The door was flung open and Avery's presence filled the silence his entrance created. She could feel the blush covering her face at her body's immediate reaction to this handsome, virile man. Every woman in the room was as enamored by him as she was, but he only had love for her.

He crossed the room and knelt beside her rocking chair. He gazed into her eyes and took her hand. He smiled as he slowly brought her palm to meet his lips and grinned mischievously at the sighs from the other women witnessing his devotion to his lovely young wife. He leaned close enough to whisper in her ear.

"See my love? You are truly a lucky woman! Even the old ones envy your good fortune at sharing my bed."

Tori chuckled and stroked the back of his silky hair.

"Yes, it's true, sweet Avery, but have you not noticed the admiring looks I've gotten from men around town?"

Avery's eyes flashed with jealousy momentarily, just until he caught himself and realized she was merely teasing him. He shared her quiet laughter, then his gaze grew more serious as he stared into her face with a look that promised he would show her just how well he could love her, later, when the house was quiet and the only sounds were those of passion.

He stood, smiled at the women assembled around Victoria, then walked to the outside of the circle. Max stood and stretched his compact body and waited for his master to rub him behind his pointed ears, just the way he liked it. Avery kindly obliged the pooch then stepped past the small canine guard.

His chest puffed with pride as he stood next to an ornate crib covered with white eyelet lace. Mindless to Max's steady gaze and the women admonishing him to leave well enough alone, he reached into the crib and picked up his sleeping son.

Avery walked back to Tori and sat on a small stood at her side. He held the baby and leaned close so his shoulder touched hers, the family circle complete. He gazed with wonder at the tiny face, soft in sleep, the long black lashes covering his cherub cheeks. Joshua's pink mouth make suckling motions as if he were nursing his mother's breast and Avery chuckled at the sight. As if in disgust at his father's apparent lack of good sense, Joshua sighed loudly, eliciting a joyful, hearty laugh from his father.

Tori's mocking glare was directed toward her husband.

"Avery, you're going to have the child spoiled rotten if you don't stop holding him all the time and laughing continuously. Joshua's going to grow up thinking the world was only created for his amusement."

"No, my sweet Victoria, with a mother like you, Joshua will grow to be strong, intelligent and loving."

Avery turned his face to look deeply into her eyes.

"How could I have been so lucky? I have the most beautiful woman alive who loves me, the world's most handsome, brilliant son, a faithful dog, and a happy home. Yes, God has truly blessed me and I never forget to thank Him every day. And I give thanks to you and your heart, Victoria, for creating the wondrous dream which became a reality."

More books by
Gloria Teague

Saturday Night Cocoa Fudge is the coming-of-age story in an era of bobby socks, poodle skirts and the freckled-faced girl that wore them. It's also about the Deep South and sweetly flawed women who taught her what she was meant to be and what she was *not* meant to be. Their corner of the world was filled with folklore, superstition, and mystical ideas. Her grandmother believed and practiced most of these, passing them onto the next generation. The little girl's life was populated with strange relatives, quirky neighbors and mysterious bible verses that could stop the flow of blood. Being a member of this bizarre family made life worth living. These people were so fiercely loyal in their love for her, for each other, she felt they deserved to have their story told.

http://www.awocbooks.com/book.cfm?b=56

Beyond the Surgeon's Touch: One Miracle Away from Death — Ami was three years old when her mother's killer attempted to murder her, too. The battle to save her life was fought by doctors and nurses, but it was only through a miraculous intervention that Ami is alive today. *Beyond the Surgeon's Touch* is filled with stories based on actual events that have been witnessed and recorded by the staff of emergency rooms and surgical suites, even in their own lives. These accounts prove that medical personnel are, after all, just human and they pray for divine assistance when trying to save a life. Sometimes those pleas are answered. These stories illustrate that miracles can, and do, happen to average people more often than you may realize.

http://www.awocbooks.com/book.cfm?b=67

Safe in the Heart of a Miracle: More True Stories of Medical Miracles — Just when it seems all is lost, that hope is gone and death is a certainty, when doctors tell a dying patient's family to make funeral arrangements, God steps in to prove he is still in charge. Wrapping his arms around a broken body, he saves what others would have lost.

Here is the sequel to *Beyond the Surgeon's Touch*. These are actual medical cases that defy logical explanation. But God's miracles have always defied man's logic and we are blessed because of it.

http://www.awocbooks.com/book.cfm?b=101

CPSIA information can be obtained at www.ICGtesting.com
Printed in the USA
LVOW130355210912

299580LV00001B/42/P